ARDENT WINGS ON JEALOUS SKIES

TALES OF CIEL
BOOK 1

Z. BENNETT LORIMER

HIGH TRESTLE
PRESS

ARDENT WINGS ON JEALOUS SKIES

Cover design by Zefanya Maega

A High Trestle Press Book
Address
Ames, IA 50010

ISBN 978-1-968122-00-3 (Ebook) | ISBN 978-1-96822-01-0 (Trade Paperback)

First Printing, November 2025
Printed in the U.S.A.

For Liz

PROLOGUE: KLAEDA

Tortuga pushed off from the Isle of Myin, flippers battering the open sky like oars. Tradewinds heaved the old Leviathan up into the stratosphere, outracing catapults and cannon fire, while shrinking Myin's shoreline snorted frustrated pillars of smoke and smoldering ash into its wake. Only the reek of it ever reached Tortuga's crew.

Captain Hekuba Klaeda tugged on the brim of her three-pointed hat, concealing the amused glint in her loamy eyes. Those eyes were too soulful for such grim work—too pretty by half, or so she'd been told.

Tortuga's mind lurked at the edge of her consciousness, a bundle of changeable emotions, ever present. The two lived in constant dialog through their bond—equals joined in lifelong debate as they goaded each other down one path or another. Klaeda could press when the moment demanded a firm hand, but Tortuga pressed back. Such was the bond between a Leviathan and its chosen Pilot.

Her crew skidded around the deck built atop Tortuga's natural shell, tending to chores and rapidly girding the riggings after the abrupt departure. The twins, Seel and Mar, circled the taffrail, pulling up ropes and mooring left to dangle in the open air. Their Avian scout, Cak, unfurled his black wings and fluttered up the ladder to the crow's nest, while First Mate Stellan barked orders over the howling winds. Only her hostler, Jaim, was missing; likely below deck preparing Tortuga's grooming.

At that thought, Tortuga's gratitude washed across the bond.

Not until we're clear, Klaeda sent back as she pushed the Leviathan to continue her climb. Tortuga complained through the bond, even as she complied with the order. However uncanny, Leviathan were living creatures and prone to exhaustion. They'd rode Tortuga hard on this run, but Klaeda couldn't rule out an Armada presence in the skies around Myin. It wouldn't serve to linger—not if doing so might jeopardize their prize.

With that in mind, she turned to her captive.

The man struggled blindly, face concealed beneath a burlap hood. Fulmina held the end of the rope she and Dindo used to hogtie his ankles to his wrists, and she jerked it cruelly. Someone had slashed the captive's leg with a saber—left a weeping gash down his thigh, ruining his pleated pants.

As Klaeda approached, Fulmina slipped her blade under the captive's chin and lifted his hooded head. Wind whipped Fulmina's limp hair against one side of her face, and Klaeda saw half a smile peeking out behind that red curtain.

"The little fop is finally acting right," Fulmina said.

"What changed?" Klaeda asked.

Fulmina withdrew her blade, gnawing the corner of her lip where a long scar that extended down her chin began. "He settled down once he felt the draft."

Dindo agreed, bald head bobbing. "Probably realized we got him up off the island. Knows the jig is up." He drew one thumb across his throat and made a strangling sound.

"Let him breathe the open air," Klaeda said.

Fulmina reached down and removed the captive's hood, revealing a squinting face shaped like a dagger with a cleft chin at its point. A bruise darkening one swollen cheekbone matched the size and shape of Dindo's meaty fist. Her captive might have been a handsome man by some standards. So defeated and bound, it was hard to tell. He had a thick coif of sandy blonde hair bound back in a high ponytail with a scrap of black ribbon. Klaeda felt a lock of her own blonde hair tickling her ear as she judged him. She tucked the errant strand back inside her hat and checked the brim once more to ensure her eyes remained shaded.

So set, she crouched before her captive and grasped him by the cleft in his chin, guiding his head to judge him in profile. With the other hand she folded back his earlobe, revealing the Celestials' proprietary brand—a broken serpent enclosed in an orb.

Klaeda released the ear with a flick and stood back up, clucking her disapproval. She projected her voice across the deck. "Looks like we got ourselves a collaborator."

The crew began to gather. This was the good part.

Klaeda tapped her chin, gaze narrowing on her captive while the audience settled in. "I used to ask collaborators *what kind of person sells out their own for the Shards*? Got a lot of answers back, too. Long ones. Short ones. Ugly lies and uglier truths. I'm a sailor first and foremost, so I always appreciate a good tall tale, but I don't ask that question anymore. You know why?"

The captive bent painfully within his bindings to meet her gaze. "I'm guessing you didn't like the answers." The Shards' elevated dialect tainted his dulcimer voice, and each syllable was like the blast of a bellows stoking Klaeda's rage. Nothing she hated more than an uppity collaborator.

"Wrong." She reached down to flick his branded ear again, making him wince. "It got *boring*. In the end, every mope I ever picked up with that little cattlemark behind their ear was either greedy or scared. So, I ask a different question now: which one are you?"

"What does it matter?" The Patrician sneered up at Klaeda. "This isn't a tribunal."

Cak's squawking from the crow's nest sent Stellan skating over with a report. "We're at 3,000 feet over meridian altitude, Captain."

Klaeda nodded. Through her bond, she sent Tortuga instructions to stop climbing and peel off anti-driftward. "You hear that, *Sire*? We're in Sky Law now." She snapped at her First Mate. "Stellan, remind me the punishment for collaborating under Sky Law?"

A rotten-toothed grin cut across Stellan's hatchet face. "Collaborators get the Long Drop, Cap'n."

The captive began struggling fruitlessly against his bindings. He looked ridiculous flopping around on her deck in his ruined Patrician blues.

Fulmina kicked him in the gut, putting a sudden end to the squirming. Shaking her head, Klaeda leaned down again and flipped open her spring knife. She fingered the whalebone handle in her gloved hand before reaching back to cut the Patrician loose.

Limbs freed, he quickly rolled onto his back and scrambled for the taffrail, nails clawing at Tortuga's deck. Dindo blocked him with his thick body, and Fulmina drew her saber to guide him back toward the waiting plank. As soon as one fumbling hand found the breach in Tortuga's taffrail, the Patrician froze.

He ventured a glance over his shoulder and began to tremble. Klaeda watched his eyes scream along the length of the plank and out to the empty sky beyond.

His head whipped around, eyes jerking back to her. "You wouldn't."

Klaeda sighed and threw up her hands. "I don't make the rules, but I do enforce 'em. You know something about that, being a Patrician and all."

The captive threw himself past Fulmina's saber into a heap at Klaeda's feet. "Mercy! I beg of you." All the sneer vanished from his expression—the haughtiness gone from his blubbering voice. "I was a good magistrate. A *just* magistrate. The plebiscite—they loved me. If I'm to be executed, I demand the Hard Drop."

Klaeda kicked his prayerful hands away, sparing her boots any further soil. She caught a sly smirk on Fulmina's face as she rubbed her chin, considering. "Hard Drop's for killers and thieves, Sire. If I let you walk that plank over land, you get off with a few moments of hurtling terror before death's sweet release." She opened her stance, projecting her voice to her assembled crew. "Is that a mercy this collaborator deserves?"

Curses and jeers rose up around her. The captive Patrician shrunk beneath the weight of a mob demanding his tortured end.

"All right, all right..." Klaeda simmered her rowdy crew. "Enough of that. As Pilot of this Leviathan and captain of this crew, Sky Law permits me to make a commutation, but you'll have to give me something if you expect me to exercise such extraordinary discretion."

"Yes!" His eyes bugged from his swollen head. The poor bastard actually thought he'd found salvation. "Anything. *Anything* that's in my power to give."

Klaeda nodded thoughtfully. She almost pitied the little prick. "What's your Gift then, Sire?"

"My—my Gift?"

"You need me to spell it?"

The question seemed to catch him off guard, but the Celestials never elevated a man to Patrician unless he was among the Gifted—Jokai-blessed to wield some divine skill or ability.

"I—I am an Alchemist."

Dindo perked up at the admission. Hard to tell by the look of him, but the pot-bellied sailor also counted himself among the Gifted—another Alchemist just like this rotten collaborator. Dindo's Gift empowered him to strain the toxins from turned food.

"Care to get more specific?" Klaeda pressed.

The Patrician's lips flapped as he stuttered through a few half-baked attempts to dissemble.

That was well enough. She was only toying with him. Klaeda knew what she had in this captive. His Gift turned worthless stones into precious gems, but the likeness was only skin deep. Beneath all the false gilt and glitter lay a flaw. She pulled one of these trinkets, a false emerald, from the hide purse at her belt and held it up to catch the sun's light. She tossed the worthless jewel into the air and in one fluid motion drew her saber, striking it in half so that both pieces landed in her captive's lap, their mundane innards exposed.

The magistrate flinched at the flash of blade. He opened one eye and looked down at the stones without moving to collect them.

"One of yours, I take it?" Klaeda felt her upper lip curling with disgust. "You don't have to answer. The question's rhetorical. This stone was used in the purchase of a map. I want you to tell me where to find the cartographer who made it. Answer me that, and we'll grant you the Hard Drop."

Mouth quivering, the captive shook his head, unable to meet the hidden gaze of his judge and executioner. "I—I don't know. I've made thousands of jewels for our hosts—"

"Our *what*?" Klaeda growled.

Realizing his mistake too late, he pressed his lips shut. "The Celestials..." he corrected. "I can't possibly—that emerald could have been spent by any of them."

Drumming her fingers, Klaeda *tsk tsked*. "That is too bad."

On her mark, Dindo hauled the captive up over escalating protests and, with one mighty heave, cast him out onto the plank. Blubbering again, the collaborator scrambled to maintain his balance as the platform wavered beneath his feet. The thin plank extended far out behind the ruffles of Tortuga's shell.

Once he steadied himself, the captive lunged back toward the deck, but Fulmina struck him with the pommel of her saber and kicked him out to the plank's edge. Howling, he dropped to his stomach and hugged the flapping plank. Klaeda watched him venture one tremulous glance at his fate then slam his eyes shut with a curse. He began muttering some insensate prayer, words lost to the winds whipping around him.

"You're balanced on a knife's edge over bare sky," Klaeda said. "You're going to spend the rest of your natural life falling through it. You're going to fall and fall and fall—until your heart stops or your organs give out from dehydration. Bad way to go, I'm afraid."

Fulmina pranced out onto the plank and poked at his whitening knuckles with the point of her blade. The crew roared with amusement. Even Klaeda couldn't resist a grin.

"Last chance, Sire. Where's the cartographer?"

"I-I don't know—I swear it!" He screamed to be heard over the winds.

Klaeda signaled Fulmina to end it, but before she swung her saber around, the collaborator raised his panicked voice again.

"I can tell you this, though! The cartographer you're looking for—he's Gifted. He makes maps that only he can read. Our hosts—*the Celestials*—they didn't just use my jewels to purchase a map. They bought the man himself. They must be keeping him at one of their palaces in the sector."

Fulmina lowered her saber and looked to Klaeda for a sign. The bastard's words had the ring of truth. What good was the map, after all, if only this Gifted cartographer could read it? How many Celestial Palaces in the sector? Maybe three—not counting Toran, of course.

"Cap'n?" Fulmina looked eager to end it.

Klaeda signaled her to hold. "Based on the information you've provided," she declared, "I hereby commute your sentence for collaborating."

A groan of disappointment from the crew.

"Bless you!" the Patrician howled over the din, still gripping the end of the plank. "Bless you!"

"*Unfortunately,*" Klaeda raised her voice over both her captive's desperate blessings and the complaints of her crew, "in the provision of that information, you've incriminated yourself for the crimes of fraud and kidnapping. The penalty is... *the Long Drop.*"

Cheers erupted anew from the crew around her. Fulmina flourished her saber theatrically and hopped back out onto the plank, thrusting the point against the captive's grasping hands.

"I won't do it!" the collaborator screamed over the celebration. "You'll have to run me through. I won't jump over bare sky."

"Jump?" Klaeda walked up to the edge of the deck. "Who said anything about jumping?"

Fulmina sheathed her saber and leapt back onto the deck. Klaeda backed away, and Dindo took her place. The Gifted sailor raised his dagger to the crew, then swept down to cut the tether anchoring the plank to Tortuga's deck. With a *snap* of broken tension, the plank tipped over its fulcrum, slamming against the side of Tortuga's shell. The impact broke the captive's desperate grip and sent him tumbling down the Leviathan's body. Everybody rushed to the taffrail to watch him shriek as he tipped over Tortuga's ruffles, hands scraping, finding nothing but empty sky.

His cries echoed long after Klaeda's crew dispersed, returning to the business of manning Tortuga. Those cries would continue for days and maybe weeks, for there was no release lurking in the blue void between the floating islands of Ciel—no sweet ground rising up to meet him. The Long Drop was torment stacked upon torment, and the Jokai stacked it all the way down.

Down, into the infinite sky.

1

EFFIE

Effie scythed through the onlookers, throwing elbows into ribs and trampling moccasined toes. She continued pushing until she reached the front of the crowd, dragging Kai behind her by the wrist. The boy stood a head shorter than her, a stature he paired with the startled disposition of a field mouse. She pretended not to hear his weak protests as he stumbled along, struggling to keep pace.

Hundreds of spectators assembled at the cliffs—the largest Ascension Ceremony in Effie's recollection, which admittedly didn't stretch back very far. Pilgrims arrived from every far-flung village in the archipelago. Aeolus sent its delegation by contracted zeppelin, while Avernus and Nimbion relied on a small local fleet of kite-ships. Even the tiny Spurs were represented, though the Spurrians could hardly afford passage on a blimp.

"Effie, wait—" Kai had fallen two steps behind, and now the other eager spectators were closing ranks, clotting the trail almost as fast as Effie could blaze it.

Groaning, she gave a straw-capped Nimbion a hard shove and marched back, grabbing Kai by the wrist to pull him the rest of the way behind her. "Do you want to miss it?" she hissed.

"I could see fine from the back..."

"You couldn't see past old Bolo's round ass. Come on. I want a good view of Vanna."

The Ascension Ceremony had always captivated Effie. She loved every bit of the annual pageantry: the village's tense energy in the build-up; the caravan across Volturnus; the sleek pod of wild dauphine gathering in the Moonflow Lagoon. Even the fleeting glimpse of their elusive Celestial host offered intrigue, and this year Effie had a personal stake in the outcome.

This year, her sister Vanna—the most Gifted Elementalist on the Isle of Volturnus—would attempt to tame a wild Leviathan.

The Jokai of Ciel didn't grant their Gifts equally. The archipelago produced a fresh crop of Elementalists every year, but the ability to command a Leviathan remained elusive. In the ten years since the first Ascension, only two Zephyri had successfully bonded one of the wild dauphine. Now Vanna would be the third; Effie felt it in her gut...

...right alongside a nagging fear. The dread knowledge that her sister's success would take her away from Volturnus—possibly forever. The Celestials whisked away the last two Pilots who proved their worth, and no one in the archipelago had heard from either one since.

Dropping Kai's arm, Effie crept up to the edge of the cliff and peered down into the bowl of the lagoon. Thin shrouds of morning mist still clung to the mossy ground around the pool where moonflow bubbled up from the heart of Volturnus. Fed by a deep spring, the lagoon danced in eddies and vortices, churning with endemic light as it coursed over the lip of the island and down into open sky.

Once a year in this sacred place, a pod of wild dauphine came to graze— a pitstop on their cyclical migration across the skies of Ciel. Leviathan like the dauphine spent their entire lives in the sky, time split between active flight and a restful state of floating torpor. True landings like Volturnus' Moonflow Lagoon were exceedingly rare.

Kai lingered several steps behind as Effie crept toward the cliffside, edging forward until she stood on the cusp of falling, her toes probing the open air over the lagoon. The fresh scent of jasmine and honeysuckle gusted upward on the canyon's warm breath. She closed her eyes and imagined herself atop a bonded dauphine, legs straddling its dorsal fin as she drove her mount across the open blue.

Kai's apprehension made no sense to her. Who wouldn't want this feeling? With one step, she could walk off the edge of the world.

She and Kai were only thirteen years old. Juveniles not yet come into their Gifts and forbidden the privilege of flight between the isles by Celestial Law. In three years, it would be their turn to Ascend, and though Effie feared losing Vanna in the intervening time, she knew that she would eventually join her. The dauphine roosted in her unconscious mind as predictably as they returned to the Moonflow Lagoon—and with much greater frequency. Her time would come. In three years, she'd reunite with Vanna on some faraway shore—wherever Leviathan Pilots go. Three years was not so long to be alone.

Effie cast her gaze out toward the horizon. She made a visor with her hand, squinting as pinpoint shadows appeared against the ceiling of gauzy clouds.

"Look!" Effie reached back, and Kai yelped as she pulled him to her side.

Once he found his footing, the undersized boy followed her lead, squinting into the rising sun. Effie pointed his chin at the approaching murmuration.

"Whoa..." Kai's eyes widened.

Matching sounds of adulation rippled behind them as the spectators standing farther back noticed the dauphine approaching. Effie counted dozens—sleek bodies barrel rolling in chaotic formation, knifing through the turbulent leeward currents with greater dexterity than a Celestial fighter. Each one was the length of a mid-sized zeppelin—and more agile, by far.

Smooth cetacean bodies resolved as the skies around Volturnus erupted with their cackling song. The alpha arrowed to the head of the pod's formation, clucking and cooing, arched jaws peeling back around its bottlenose in a rictus grin. She grabbed Kai's hand, and this time he did not resist. They both watched the dauphine make landfall.

The creatures came in hues ranging from blue and gray to pink and violet. They navigated the skies by the grace of two dorsal fins, four ruffled flippers, and a star-fluked tail that spun like a propeller.

Several of the dauphine broke from the pod's murmuration at the first sign of land. They dove straight for the lagoon, submerging their massive bodies only to burst free moments later spouting buoyant ether from their blowholes. Others seemed timid, content to bask on the edge of the lagoon in floating torpor. A third cohort waited patiently just beyond the island's demesne, pacing across bare sky or bathing in the eternal falls.

The pod's pink alpha floated lazily at the center of the lagoon, rotating between its back and its white belly, cooing playfully at its peers. It was a magnificent specimen—as long as the zeppelin that carried the spectators from Aeolus. Effie nearly tripped off the cliff's edge watching the dauphine sun itself. When she stumbled, Kai caught her by the shirt. She smiled back at him sheepishly and acquiesced to a safer vantage.

Soon after the dauphine arrived, the new cohort of Ascendants emerged into the canyon from a cave inside the cliffs. Effie only saw the tops of their heads as they moved reticently into view, none yet daring to make the moonflow's approach. She searched the figures below and noticed Kai doing the same. Twenty-one young Zephyri, each selected to set their Gifts against the greatest test in Ciel. A full fifteen of the year's cohort came from their home island of Volturnus, and Effie knew them all by name. Many wore the gray wing-collared uniform of the island's Dragoon Corps.

The dragoons were all Elementalists—Zephyri Gifted to shape the winds and fly unaided between the isles. They provided a kind of provincial service corps, passing messages and responding to emergencies around the archipelago. The dragoons used to be the first line of defense against smuggling and piracy, though that function had been taken up by the Celestial Armada in the years since their host's arrival.

Both successful Ascendants had come through the corps. To hear the older villagers tell it, both young Pilots had the potential to make Wing Commander if they hadn't been snatched away to a greater destiny. Similar things were said of Vanna.

"There she is." Kai pointed down into the lagoon.

Effie tracked Kai's gesture to a lone dragoon lingering near the back of the gaggle with the same violet hair as Effie—the same plum highlights trailing from the roots. Effie let her hair grow long, but Vanna cut hers in a short bob that pleasantly framed her face. She had a woman's figure already, and Effie envied her curves, trapped as she was in the gawky frame of adolescence.

Why wasn't she jockeying for position? Some of the other Ascendants seemed to be doing just that. A tall, muscular boy with messy black hair had already claimed the pull position, beating back the smaller members of his cohort as they crowded the lagoon's approach. His knit poncho, stitched with the six-pointed star of the Spurs, flapped wildly behind him like a cape. Effie wanted to shout down to Vanna but knew her voice would be lost in the noise from the crowd.

"She looks like our host's statue in the village square," Kai said. "She looks ready."

Effie grunted. Vanna did look like a statue, but was she petrified or poised?

In that moment, Vanna glanced back over her shoulder and up the cliffside. She might have imagined it, but Effie thought they made eye contact —that she saw her sister nod and wink. Effie envisioned a sly smile onto her sister's face, the one that exposed her crooked tooth—just the kind of imperfection that only made Vanna more beautiful.

Another wave of excitement passed over the crowd. Expectant voices bubbled up, but where the clamor around the dauphine's arrival had been exultant, this latest round was more muted, seasoned with fear.

From the pathway north to Aquilon's Landing, a regal carriage pulled by six hippocampi soared into view. The hippocampi were not Leviathan. They were of a size with a common terrestrial horse and could only float short distances over solid ground. Six Patrician lords rode these domesticated beasts—two men and two women approaching or arrived at middle age and one elder woman with silver hair that flowed behind her on her mount's draft. Effie only recognized one of them at a distance: Sire Ansel, the square-jawed Governor of Volturnus.

The carriage pulled to a stop across the canyon. As one, the Zephyri crowd watched the Patricians dismount and hobble their hippocampi. Sire Ansel proceeded up to the carriage and opened its gilt-framed door, folding one arm behind his back and bowing the gray-streaked black of his head.

Her Lightness the Celestial Kelestina, Host of the Zephyr Isles, took the offered hand and stepped down from her floating carriage to greet her guests. She looked much like her marble statue in the village square— elegant, chiseled, and remote, with reedy limbs and unblemished, alabaster skin. Her tilted eyes glowed green, accented by a sharp smoky tint applied in the shape of wings. Like all Celestials, Kelestina was hairless. Her skull instead drew back into a bundle of jagged points like broken quartz—a permanent crown the Jokai fashioned to adorn the chosen race. Kelestina rarely found occasion to come down from her palace on the Island of Aquilon, but she never missed an annual Ascension.

The Celestial's appearance silenced the crowd.

"*Pssst... Effie!*"

Effie felt a tug on her skirt and looked down to discover that Kai had dropped to one knee. Then she looked around and realized *everyone* was kneeling. With an embarrassed squeak, she dropped to the ground beside him.

One of the younger Patricians played herald, while Governor Ansel stood barrel-chested beside his Lady Host. "Her Lightness the Celestial Kelestina, Host of the Zephyr Isles, and Lady Paramount of Aquilon Palace."

Kelestina raised her hands in response to her introduction, long fingers extended so the razor tips of her teardrop nails caught the morning sun. "Rise, my honored guests." Her alto voice rang like a bell. It carried across the canyon's gulf, musical and resonant. "We gather on the occasion of the dauphine's sojourn to bear witness to the Eleventh Ascension of the Zephyr Isles."

Polite cheers from the crowd rose in response to the milestone. Effie applauded dutifully along.

"Since my court arrived on Aquilon to deliver these islands from perdition, we have used this ceremony not only to identify the rare Gift required to pilot Leviathan, but to mark the maturation of your sons and daughters —to induct them into their majority as accounted members of the Celestial plebiscite. I take this moment to acknowledge those among us who arrive bereft of Gifts yet may still contribute as valued members of our great society."

More cheers met this pronouncement. Effie saw a smattering of sixteen-year-old Zephyri sprinkled throughout the crowd. Adjacent friends and family members gave them hugs and ruffled heads. Older siblings and younger peers offered playful shots to the arm. It all felt too much like a consolation to Effie—a weak taste of the honor bestowed on the Ascendants below.

Poor bastards. Effie couldn't imagine a worse fate than standing atop these cliffs in the year of her majority, so worthless that she didn't even merit a chance to *test* herself against the wild dauphine. Kelestina's acknowledgement was kind, but empty.

As the congratulations receded, Kelestina turned her attention to the Ascendants waiting below. Effie spared another glance for Vanna at the bottom of the canyon. Her sister craned her neck like the rest of her cohort, watching their host's presentation from the banks of the lagoon.

Without any further ceremony, Kelestina returned to her carriage, and her Patrician attendants mounted their hippocampi. The procession took off from its cliffside landing and plunged down into canyon. At the bottom, Kelestina exited her carriage again and spoke words intended only for the Ascendants. Effie watched them gather around their host, some standing close enough to touch her. She noticed Vanna still lurking near the back of the pack and found herself *willing* her sister to push closer—to soak up every sensory detail of her life's pinnacle moment. Her sister did no such thing, content to linger on the outskirts of her cohort.

The briefing concluded, and Kelestina offered her blessing to each of the Ascendants in turn before sending them back to the lagoon's approach to form an orderly queue.

The Spurrian boy in the poncho was the first to attempt the Leviathan. He crept up to the edge of the lagoon and plunged through the ether to challenge the floating alpha. He barely got within ten feet of the dauphine before the creature lurched out, flourishing its bottlenose like a lance. The boy dodged the first thrust, but the alpha caught him with the broad side of its nose on the backswing, tossing him several feet through the air. He landed with a thump on the opposite shore followed by a gasp of disappointment from the crowd.

Rejection. *And so it begins.*

Effie watched the Ascension proceed with failure after failure. None of the other Ascendants dared approach the pod's ill-tempered alpha, but they had no better luck with the subordinates. A few of the uniformed dragoons used their Gifts to glide out beyond the edge of the island, courting the younger specimens that lingered offshore. One young woman from Aeolus with pink hair pinned in a complicated bun managed to draw one of these floating dauphine out from the moonflow falls. The Aeolian approached on a vortex of air, and the dauphine permitted it—intrigued by the mechanics of her Gift. It allowed the girl to touch its smooth brow, and the spectators drew a simultaneous gasp. The girl no doubt thought she had it made. She bowed to the creature, but as soon as she attempted to mount, the Leviathan bent its back like a massive bow and bucked her back into the lagoon. The spectators groaned in their shared voice as the most promising prospect yet paddled back to shore, pink Aeolian bun disheveled.

Vanna waited until the very end—the last Ascendant to make her approach. Effie fumbled for Kai's hand again, which he accepted willingly.

They watched Vanna pace the edge of the lagoon, judging each dauphine from a safe distance. She stared at her options intently, taking each creature's measure. One of the shy Leviathan noticed her display and crossed the island's threshold to plop itself down in the ether. Vanna knelt, testing the moonflow in front of this dauphine with her fingers, waiting for the creature to come to her.

The standoff seemed to stretch an eternity. Vanna held her ground, splashing her hand in the lagoon, forcing eye contact on the wading dauphine. At last, the creature relented and began swimming toward her, propelled by its spinning flukes. With a dip of its flippers, it turned its broadside to the shore and brought one gleaming eye level with Vanna.

In that moment, all the hot blood in Effie's veins turned to ice. Vanna was the most Gifted Elementalist in a generation—the future of the Volturnian dragoons. She'd never failed at anything before—not in Effie's recollection. What were the chances she'd start failing now? Even when Effie claimed her own Leviathan in three years' time, there was no guarantee she'd be reunited with Vanna. No one knew what happened after the Celestials took the successful Ascendants away. No one knew where the Pilots went or what they became.

She watched the gap close between her sister and that dauphine's soulful eye, and she saw their lives together shrinking away.

"No."

Kai looked up at her. She hadn't intended to say it out loud.

Please.

In the lagoon below, Vanna reached out to touch the dauphine.

The creature let her.

Don't take her away.

Vanna slid her hands along the dauphine's broad flank, patted one flipper then drew up, preparing to mount. The dauphine cooed in response...

...then it rolled to its side and—with that same muscular flipper—swatted Vanna against the rocky cliff.

Effie realized she hadn't been breathing. Lightheaded, she allowed herself to resume, watching as her sister gingerly hoisted herself up off the ground, rubbing her tender backside. Vanna looked back at all the other failed Ascendants, and this time Effie did see that snaggle-toothed grin. Sweeping violet bangs out of her eyes, Vanna shrugged up at the spectators, and the tension of the moment shattered. Peals of laughter rolled over the crowd.

Kai wasn't laughing, but he smiled ear to ear. He wouldn't have wanted to lose Vanna, either. "Sorry, Eff. I know you thought she'd be the one."

Effie tried to hide her relief, but something in the ease of Kai's expression marked her failure.

In the aftermath, Effie found herself watching Kelestina, returned to the clifftop to call the day's ceremony to a close. It was so difficult to tell from such a distance and on such a cyclopean face, but she thought she saw a new set to their host's smoky eyes—a subtle twist of discontent on those crystalline Celestial lips.

Effie never forgot that look.

2

EFFIE

The failed Ascendants joined their families atop the cliffs after the ceremony. Vanna found Effie and Kai amid the confusion of hugs and affectionate chatter.

"You were so close," Kai exclaimed.

"Was I?" Vanna's smile radiated warmth, but Effie knew her sister well enough to see the thin scaffolding of relief propping up the veneer. Not a hint of disappointment, though. Effie didn't quite know what to make of it.

"You were," Kai said. "Closer than anybody else, at least."

Vanna perched her hands on her hips and raised her eyebrows behind a purple curtain of tousled bangs. "Didn't feel that way in the moment."

"There's no such thing as close," Effie interjected. "You're either bonded to a Leviathan or you're not." Even to her own ears, she sounded peevish.

"Just so," Vanna agreed, unbothered by or unaware of her sister's attitude. "Come on. I'm half starved." She gestured for Kai and Effie to follow and plodded off toward a gathering of Volturnian dragoons.

The Zephyri spectators formed tribal circles and shared a picnic meal of bread, hard cheeses and smoked meat—all of it carried along with the caravan from the village on the southern end of Volturnus. Everyone crossed Volturnus by wagon or on foot, as much out of necessity as by tradition. The best landings on the island abutted the village, and the road to the lagoon crossed a thin strip of jungle that offered no easy descent.

Kelestina glided away with her retinue of Patrician lords long before the festivities commenced. Effie selfishly hoped to get a closer look at their host, but Kelestina must have known she made everybody nervous. Not a soul in the archipelago would have been able to eat in the Celestial's presence.

The Volturnian circle quickly decayed into branches and cliques. Effie, Kai, and Vanna sat off the main spur among a few young dragoons all dressed in their collared flight suits, breast patches displaying the dandelion Crest of Zephyr and the curling east wind of Volturnus. A broad-shouldered young man two years older than Vanna wore a third bronze-wing patch indicating the rank of Draft Lieutenant. His name was Kendy, and his rank placed him in charge of training the cadets.

Kendy handed Vanna a basket of cheeses and cured meat to share with Kai and Effie. "Condolences," he said, though the sparkle in his eye undermined the sentiment. "Maybe too soon, but the Celestials' loss is the dragoons' gain."

"Damn right." Vanna snatched the basket from his outstretched hand and immediately pulled out a wedge of cheese to snack on. "What do I need with a Leviathan, anyway? Much more comfortable flying on my own wings, thank you." Touching her Gift, Vanna sent a gust of wind to slam shut the basket and pumped her eyebrows at Kendy.

Just a moment ago, Effie had prayed for her sister to fail the Ascension, but Vanna's attitude itched like a splinter lodged under her skin. She seemed so *dismissive.* "They'd teach you, you know," she blurted out. Vanna and Kendy both looked down at her. "The Celestials. They'd *teach* you to pilot Leviathan. What you're doing with your Gift—it's not even flying. Not really. You just glide on the wind."

Kendy's eyebrows knit together across his brow, but the sharp words didn't pierce Vanna's good humor. She took another bite of cheese and handed the rest of the wedge to Effie. "Eat something. You're getting cranky."

Effie pouted for the rest of the morning. She watched Vanna move about the gathering, exchanging jokes and false condolences with Volturnians from all walks. Kai followed her around the circle like a trained Avian, beaming up at Vanna and plucking bites from the picnic basket as they were offered. Scoffing, Effie looked around for better amusements.

A few dozen Zephyri still hung around the cliff's edge, raptured by the dauphine enjoying their leisure as they lingered around the lagoon. By sunset the Leviathan would all be gone, vanished from skies around Volturnus for another year.

Elsewhere, she saw the Nimbions in their straw hats and yellow capes beginning to pack up their wares to get on with the long march back to their landing. The Aeolians busied themselves doing the same. Four Spurrian women who arrived in a dilapidated kite-ship to accompany their lone Ascendant had latched onto a circle of Aeolian dragoons in matching flight suits. They stuck out like mating peacocks in their brightly colored dresses with long skirts that ran all the way down to their toes. Effie rolled her eyes at the dragoons' clumsy efforts to jockey for the Spurrians' attention. She searched for their Ascendant, but he wasn't around. It wasn't until an Avernian cart rolled out of the way that she spotted the back of a knit poncho flapping in the canyon breeze. The Spurrian Ascendant stood along the cliff's edge, still watching the Leviathan.

Effie spared Vanna and Kai a quick glance—saw them locked in conversation with three other cadet dragoons. Vanna cracked a joke that bent the others with laughter. Stuffing the last handful of bread and cheese in her mouth, Effie pushed herself to her feet and stomped over to talk to the Spurrian.

Up close, the boy seemed massive—wider than any of the Volturnian Ascendants and taller than Kendy by a head. "Hey," she said, sidling up beside him.

He glanced her way, sniffed, then turned back to the lagoon. Frowning, Effie planted herself next to him and watched the grazing dauphine.

The awkward silence stretched on, but anything was better than watching Vanna hold court. Kai could lap at her heels all he wanted, but the thought of joining him made her more than a little nauseated. After a few more minutes passed, the Spurrian spared her another glance. A mop of black hair covered one eye, but the other glowed like molten gold. "Do you want something?" he asked in a thick western drawl.

Effie suddenly felt a foolish child wielding her stick-slim figure next to this towering hemlock of a man. What would Vanna do in this situation? She wouldn't cower, that's for sure.

"I wanted to say how impressed I was—with you, I mean." Her words seemed to surprise the Spurrian. He straightened and turned away from the dauphine to give Effie his full attention. "It doesn't seem like anyone else here even cares, but you cared," she continued. "You walked right up to the pod's alpha and offered yourself to bond. I'm sure you'll make a fine dragoon."

The boy set his fists on his hips and pressed his lips together in a face half-questioning, half-mocking. "I'm no dragoon," he said.

"No?"

He shook his head.

"Aren't you an Elementalist?" Effie pried.

He considered the question, tongue planted in his chiseled cheek. Without answering, he gestured out over the Moonflow Lagoon. "I'm a sailor without a ship. This would have been an easy path, but I don't care what the *Shards* think—" Effie flinched at the crass reference to their host. "I'm going to find my way onto a Leviathan... one way or another." He turned back to the dauphine, and this time Effie knew the sheen in his golden eye for longing. She'd worn that same look herself a time or two.

"I'm Effie Strait," she said. "From Volturnus."

"I didn't ask."

She scowled at him. "You're not very friendly."

That caught his attention again. He pressed his lips back together in that almost-smile and flipped his hair, briefly revealing his other eye.

Effie bit back a gasp.

The eye looked nothing like its counterpart—pupil and iris red upon darker red, with concentric circular markings extending across his sclera. Angry veins shot through the whole design. He cast that uneven gaze out over the celebrants and grunted. "Looks like my sisters are finished flirting." Effie clocked the four women approaching from the Aeolian circle. "We'll be heading back, then. It's an uneasy ride out to the Spurs."

"I've never been," Effie said. "But as soon as I get my Gift, I'm going to visit all the Zephyr Isles—even the Spurs."

He nodded. "I bet you will at that." He left to intercept his sisters.

Effie watched his poncho receding. *What a strange boy.* Just as she resigned herself to returning to Vanna and Kai, he turned back around to face her.

"My name's Javion," he said. "My island is not such a big place. When you do make it out to the Spurs, look for me. I'll be the tall one." He placed a flat hand atop his head jokingly. "Don't be long, though. I'm a sailor, and sailors never wait."

3

EFFIE

The Volturnians were the last to pull up their camp and pack their wagons. Some of the elderly rode along with the packed-out trash and supplies. Their caravan intercepted a favorable tailwind after crossing the jungle, and some of the dragoons took flight. Most of the archipelago's dragoons had to work with what the weather provided, but the strongest Elementalists could impose their will upon the air itself. They called this rare skill "windshaping," and Vanna had it in spades.

Vanna could have flown off with her cohort, but she elected to walk behind the wagons with Effie. It was a half-day's journey on foot from the lagoon to the outlying farms and orchards around the village. With such a late start, the Volturnians weren't likely to reach succor before dark. Effie suspected her sister intentionally held them toward the back of the caravan. Volturnus was a safe island—and it had become even safer under Celestial control—but they'd had issues in the past with brigands and even piracy. The dragoons ran their patrols, but no one liked to get caught beyond the village outskirts after dark. It was just like her sister to quietly take it upon herself to see the stragglers to safety.

Kai broke off early, eager to get back in time to help his uncle at the bakery with their evening chores. That left Effie and Vanna alone for the first time all day.

"We'll have to start moving our things tomorrow," Vanna said, breaking a prolonged silence. "Kendy and the dragoons helped clean up the house to get it ready for us."

"Oh." Effie knew this already. She'd been by their old family cottage every day in the weeks leading up to the Ascension. Vanna was an adult now, so the two girls could be trusted to live on their own in the house their parents built. The home had been vacant for the last eleven years.

Vanna bumped her sister with her hip. "What's crawled up your skirt?"

"Nothing," Effie answered too quickly. She plucked at her hemline, dodging Vanna's second attempt with her hip.

"Hoping you'd be rid of me? Is that it?" She cocked an eyebrow in Effie's direction, mischief in her voice. "Or maybe you'd rather spend another three years sharing bunk space in the longhouse?"

"No!" Effie hadn't meant to raise her voice—or maybe she had. "No," she said more quietly, cheeks flushed. "Nothing like that. I just don't understand."

"What don't you understand?"

"I don't understand how you can brush this whole thing off! You failed, Vanna. Everyone on Volturnus thought you would be the one to bond a Leviathan, and you didn't. The dauphine cast you away like everyone else."

Vanna tossed her head in the air, shaking out her purple bob. "Who cares?"

The question stopped Effie in her tracks. "I thought *you* would care."

"Well, I don't."

Effie gaped at her sister. "You expect me to believe that? I once watched you chug raw goat's milk against every boy in the longhouse until you were vomiting out your nose. You're competitive—about *everything*."

They both planted their feet as the caravan continued along, receding into the distance. "I don't want to pilot a Leviathan, Eff. I'm happy here with the dragoons—protecting Volturnus. Protecting *you*."

"In three more years, I won't need your protection. And our host protects Volturnus. You could have piloted a fighter in the Armada. You could have been raised to Patrician. Now you're just...nobody."

"Nobody, huh?"

As soon as she said it, she wanted it back. Effie shut her mouth before she did any more damage.

Vanna crossed her arms and drummed her fingers against the angular elbow of her flight suit. "Maybe the Celestials do keep us safe. I'm not so sure—" She cut herself off, thinking. "You're right, though. I won't ever sail the skies of Ciel—not any further than Grenport, at least. I won't be some Patrician lady telling people what to do from my gaudy manse. But that makes me free to govern my own life—to decide which people I love and protect. If I had the Gift of piloting Leviathan, Kelestina could have sent me anywhere on the face of Ciel. Why would I want that when everyone I care about is right here? Being nobody has its advantages."

The caravan disappeared beyond a short hill. Vanna didn't seem to notice. She was looking back at Effie, head pointed down the path to the Moonflow Lagoon and the pod of wild dauphine too stubborn to be tamed.

Effie remembered her muttered prayer for Vanna to fail, and the last embers of her outrage guttered, suffocated by shame. "You can't save mom and dad," she said.

Finally, Vanna's confident mask cracked. For the second time, Effie cursed her sharp tongue.

"Come on." Vanna motioned Effie onward. "Let's catch up."

They walked in silence again. The whole time, Effie wished she hadn't mentioned their parents. She wished she hadn't said anything at all. Why couldn't she just let Vanna be happy?

It was nearly dusk when they next sighted the caravan.

"I know I can't save them," Vanna said, finally breaking the blister of silence between them. "But *he's* still out there."

She didn't have to name *him*. Effie understood who she meant.

4

EFFIE

Before the Celestials, piracy plagued the trade routes between the Zephyr Isles. Petty crews piloting kite-ships and steam-powered reavers harried the merchant fleets and trolley lines carrying goods and people to and fro across the archipelago. The dragoons fought a constant war to police the skies around the islands, and they saw success, until an ignominious reaver arrived on their shores—a villain who put all those petty crews of cutthroats and thieves in bloody perspective.

Maug the Butcher. His name became a curse from the shoals of Nimbion to the distant Spurs. Even those too young to remember his attack knew enough to fear its very mention. The Butcher was a Gifted pilot bonded to a Leviathan skate named Devil Ray. He struck without warning, sailing into the archipelago in late autumn against the prevailing winds. He bombarded the Islands of Aeolus and Avernus just after harvest, killing hundreds and stealing their valuable crops. These brutal attacks left the remnant villagers to starve as they picked up the pieces of their broken lives.

Volturnus had less than a day's warning before Maug set his sights on the Zephyr Isles' crown jewel. The dragoons fought valiantly, but they were outmatched—mere gadflies against the deep-sky pirate and his armored skate. Maug and his crew made landfall, pillaging for weeks around the outlying farms and granaries, sacking the proud silo where the Volturnian gatherers collected their annual moonberry crop.

At the time, Kai's father, Imani, served as Wing Commander of Volturnus. He rallied the surviving dragoons and assembled the corps for one final push—a desperate attempt to drive the pirates from their shores. A battered wing from Aeolus and Avernus joined in support, but Maug had already retreated to his Leviathan. From the iron deck of Devil Ray, he swatted the dragoons out of the sky like gnats. Imani perished in the failed assault, as did so many others—Effie and Vanna's own father, Errol, among them.

Effie was only two years old at the time. Her true recollection amounted to a bundle of inchoate images and emotions: the black swoop of Devil Ray's shadow cutting across the land; a muddy tableau of decimated dragoons retreating to the village; a glimpse of two cadets holding a young comrade who would never walk again. She remembered sitting on a bed beside her sister, struggling to understand as their mother, Vera, explained that their father wouldn't be coming home—not ever again. Vera was also a dragoon—the draft lieutenant left in command of the village's reserve force. Effie's most salient memory of the day wasn't those glimpses of the injured or even the loss of her father. It was the burning panic she felt the moment her mother left them at the longhouse among the crying masses of Volturnian children—newly orphaned or about to be. It was the sight of Vanna's tear-streaked face, the way it set Effie weeping in great gasping sobs that made her throat burn and her stomach clench in angry knots.

A decade of whispered stories from that dark time filled in the gaps of her memory. Devil Ray descended on the village. Volturnus was spared the bombardment that shattered Aeolus and Avernus, but only because the pirate butcher sought to take the sprawling settlement for his own. To hear it told, Vera's dragoons put up a stolid resistance. It took Maug's crew three days to cut their way into the heart of the village, and when they finally broke through, it was over Vera's corpse that they entered the town square.

Beaten, the Volturnians stood down. The elders bent the knee to their conqueror, but Maug wasn't interested in rule. His crew began a methodical sack of the village, breaking down doors to steal valuables and drag the island's nubile sons and daughters away to unspeakable fates. The longhouse, they left untouched, and if there was one mercy from this hideous chapter, that was it. Effie had but one image of the Butcher himself, a demon's face, black-bearded and cross-hatched with scars. She remembered the sweet smell of his breath and the horrifying intelligence alight in his powder-blue eyes. He worked those eyes over the longhouse orphans appraisingly.

"Too young," he said to his murderous crew before moving on.

The nightmare might have continued indefinitely, a torment from which the Zephyr Isles would never wake, but salvation was already mounted and on its course. The Celestials arrived with an Armada squadron of angular fighters led by Leviathan warships. The battle over Volturnus lasted half a day. That was how long it took the Celestials to dislodge Maug from the village and chase his Devil Ray out of the archipelago's skies. After their operation concluded, Kelestina arrived in the village at the head of a procession of Patrician lords and ladies and Armada pilots of every stripe. They'd captured a dozen members of Maug the Butcher's crew. Their future host and ruler presented their prizes to the traumatized villagers and delivered her judgment in the public square. The children from the longhouse were brought forward to watch, for who could be more deserving of justice than the children orphaned in the pirate's weeks-long attack.

Kelestina unveiled her own Gift, then. It was the only time Effie had seen such a power deployed, before or since. The Celestial bent her crystalline head over each captive and pressed one pointed fingernail against their flesh, puncturing their chests. She drew their souls from their bodies like poison from a wound. The pirates convulsed as their lifeforce streamed out of them, siphoned essences collecting like ebbs of moonflow to be scattered on the Volturnian winds. With the captives disposed, Kelestina addressed the village.

"The criminal Maug has been cast from your skies, but he will return—and he will not be the only one. These lands are too rich to avoid unwanted attention, and your Gifts, however bountiful, will not be enough to deter those who would do you harm. These are dangerous times in Ciel. Take a night and a day to bury your dead. Mourn what you have lost. When I return, we will discuss the price of your protection."

Kelestina returned, as promised. The council of elders who ruled the islands until that day met with the Celestial behind closed doors. When they returned, all the people of the archipelago became subjects of the Crystal Throne—members of the plebiscite.

The Armada left Volturnus soon after the negotiations concluded, though Kelestina assured the elders they would be available to defend the islands if ever she made the call. Kelestina remained, as did a small cohort of Patrician functionaries. She took the underpopulated northern island of Aquilon as her high seat and began construction of the crystal palace that now stood at its highest point, visible to the naked eye from the northern promontories of Volturnus.

She designated Patrician lords to govern each island in the archipelago. Sire Ansel conscripted a hundred laborers from the Volturnian plebiscite to build his manse on a small hill outside the village. That hilltop had been home to a stone shrine of the Jokai where Volturnians wed. The whole of it had to be razed to make way.

The Celestials introduced the Ascension Ceremony that same year, and now the anticipation of that rite shaped every aspect of childhood in the Zephyrs. Effie hardly remembered life on her island before the Celestials arrived, but she knew what it was like *now*. For all the tithing and conscription, the benefits were clear.

Kelestina's prophesied disaster never came to pass. The mere presence of a Celestial host kept even Leviathan pirates like Maug the Butcher at bay.

The archipelago was safe.

5

EFFIE

Seasons changed on Volturnus. The harvest came in, and the governor's tax collectors descended upon the village to weigh and extract the Celestials' tithe. Fields lay fallow through the isles' short, cool winter, and before long, it was time again for planting. The cycle repeated itself, as surely as the navigation stars processed along the arc of the firmament, and with each repetition, Effie grew up.

By the time she turned fifteen, her body had begun filling out at the top and bottom in a close approximation of her sister's curves. She was still the thinner of the two Strait sisters, but Effie retained a softness to her form—something Vanna's diligent training regimen had sanded away. She kept her violet hair long, in part to preserve some fleeting sense of her own identity.

Kai caught up to Effie's height within months of Vanna's Ascension. By the time their fifteenth summer arrived, he'd outstripped her by a full head. The growth spurt left him lanky, with gangly limbs he hadn't quite learned to control. His face had begun to harden into a more masculine shape with a strong, square jaw and prominent cheekbones set beneath his guileless eyes. Neither one of them had manifested a Gift yet, so they spent their days at work in the fields with the rest of the plebiscite. On occasion, Kai received dispensation to help his uncle with the village bakery, but no such privilege was forthcoming during harvest season. They usually volunteered to collect moonberries, a task that took them away from the village and far from the censors' watchful eyes.

Moonberries only grew in one wild grove northwest of the village where sheer cliffs on three sides shielded the dark-leafed hedges from all but a few hours of sunlight each day. The hedges themselves grew tall and ragged, clawing their way up the jagged lines of shade, thirty feet high in some places. Thick bunches of black, serrated leaves sprouted year-round from thorny branches. In the clutches of each sharp tangle sat a single azure berry the size of a baby's fist. The uncooked fruit tasted bitter and vaguely foul, like a lemon left to turn on the tree. Their real value lay in the juice that the village apothecaries extracted from each season's harvest. From that juice, the apothecaries mixed their Nectar, the island's most valuable export. A single vial of Nectar had the ability to nourish a person for days on end without any additional food or water. For the Gifted, the effect was even more pronounced, and it came with a natural enhancement to their Jokai-blessed abilities.

Kelestina's magistrates kept a close eye on the moonberry harvest and imposed strict controls on the sale of Nectar. The older apothecaries remembered the days before their host arrived and liked to grumble about the obligation, but Effie didn't have ears for it. As far as she was concerned, Kelestina and her Leviathan Armada could make better use of such a boon than anyone else on the Zephyr Isles.

Effie tossed her half-filled cask of moonberries to the ground and lay down in the shadow of the cliffs. They'd nearly cleared all the berries within arm's reach, and she didn't see the need to overextend herself. Instead, she watched Kai's back muscles ripple beneath his sweaty shirt as he extended those goofy arms to pry a distant berry.

Grunting as he pushed up on his toes, Kai finally fumbled a grip around his quarry and managed to pluck it loose. He admired the fruit triumphantly before tossing it into his cask with all the rest. He moved further down the row, but as he reached for the next one, he clocked Effie taking a load off on a shady knoll, hands clasped behind her head, leg crossed over one knee as she idly kicked her foot. He set his cask down and wiped his brow.

"Calling it a day, Eff?"

She extended her palms to him, moaning lugubriously. "My hands—they ache! I'm not cut out for this sort of labor."

"You think you'll have it any easier with the dragoons?"

Effie sprang up on her backside. "That's different and you know it. This is scut work. We're only wasting away out here because our Gifts haven't manifested yet. No one expects an Elementalist to wither out in the fields." She looked down at her palms, hatched with burning scratches from the hedge's thorns. "You see this?" She held them up again to Kai. "I'm mutilated."

"You're the one who wanted to come out here," Kai countered.

"Only because there's no one watching us! Sire Ansel's staff can't be everywhere at once."

Kai shook his head and returned to his picking.

"Like you'll still come out here to pick berries after your Gift manifests," Effie chided. "I'll be sure to look for you gusting yourself up the cliff-side, clearing out all those hard-to-reach places."

He stopped again, stomped over to where Effie was sitting, and threw his cask down next to hers. His vessel overflowed with moonberries, a stark contrast with her own underwhelming haul. "Nothing wrong with honest work," he said.

She'd been ready with another quip, but the strain in his voice gave her pause. "No," she agreed. "There's nothing wrong with it. But we're destined for bigger things."

"Maybe..." He turned away from her, shielding his eyes.

"What is it?"

He shook his head. When he spoke again, his voice cracked. "We're fifteen, Eff. Why haven't we manifested? Oh, I'm sure you'll get yours. Your family's been Gifted as far back as the elders can remember, but me? My father was the first Elementalist in five generations, and my mother couldn't spin enough wind to blow out a candle. *Jokai fend,* my uncle's the village baker!" He looked at his own scratched hands, flushed with heat and densely calloused, fingers long as plantains. "What if my Gift never manifests? What if I'm *not* an Elementalist?"

Tears began to pool in the corners of Kai's eyes. Effie stood up and placed one hand on his shoulder. His sweaty shirt clung to his back, sticking to her hands as she felt his muscles contracting with silent sobs. "Don't talk like that. We're just late bloomers, is all. My mother was sixteen-and-a-day when she manifested, and she was as Gifted as Vanna, to hear it told."

"You never worry." It wasn't a question.

"What's to worry about? Like you said, the Gift's in my blood. It's in yours, too. Maybe not as strong, but a Gifted parent increases your chances tenfold."

He sniffed and wiped the tears from his cheeks with those awkward hands. Puffy eyes turned to her. Then, he did something she wasn't prepared for.

He bent down and kissed her.

She felt his lips moving between hers, pushing them apart as his tongue glanced off her teeth and mingled with her own. The perspiration on his upper lip tickled her nose as she inhaled the earthy scent of him. It only lasted a heartbeat.

When they drew apart, he was still holding her, and she let her own hands slide down to his strong forearms. They stared at each other in that position, breathless and awed by the sudden change in the flavor of their relationship.

"If it turns out I'm not Gifted and I spend the rest of my days at my uncle's kiln, will you still have time for me, Effie Strait?"

The question roused her from the romantic trance. "All the time I have to give," she lied.

But some lies are also true.

6

EFFIE

Effie declined to return to work that day, and Kai had to share his moonberry harvest so she wouldn't return with a half-full cask and risk the censor's inspection. They didn't kiss again on the long walk home, though as the sun began to set over the distant shore of Avernus, he did reach down to hold her hand.

They delivered their casks just before dusk and, famished, made straight for Effie and Vanna's home. They burst through the cottage door flirting deliriously, both ripe from the hike and the day's labor. They found Kendy standing over Vanna, who was seated at the kitchen table. The dragoons sat suspiciously close together, and Effie thought Vanna leaned into Kendy a little more than the conversation required. She realized they were both looking down at a square-cut sheet of bleached parchment —the type of stationary favored by the Celestials and their Patrician nobility.

"Hello?" Effie prompted.

Vanna glanced up at Effie and Kai, but her mind lingered elsewhere.

"Effie! Kai!" Kendy's grin was so bright it made Effie want to shield her eyes. The dragoon lieutenant was a man grown now, with a thick strip of black hair he kept high and tight, shaved with a razor around the sides and back. The shadow of evening stubble darkening his square jaw did little to dull his beaming expression.

Vanna smiled distractedly, then returned to the parchment missive as a kettle left overlong to boil whistled for attention.

"Is somebody going to get that?" Effie asked.

Kai took a step back toward the door, tugging her wrist. "Maybe we should come back later, Eff."

"No." Vanna stood up and moved the kettle off the wood-burning stove. "Sit."

Kai and Effie looked at each other and took the offered seats.

Kendy leaned away from the kitchen table and crossed his arms, prodding Vanna with his eyes. "Well? Are you going to tell them the good news, or am I?"

Vanna scowled at him.

"What's in the letter?" Effie asked.

"It's from Sire Ansel," Vanna answered evasively.

Effie strained over the table to peer at its contents. She saw the stamp of a broken serpent inside a circle—Kelestina's Celestial seal.

"It's a letter of appointment," Kendy clarified. "Your sister has been promoted to Draft Lieutenant of the Volturnus Dragoons. She managed it even younger than I did, but we won't let it go to her head."

Effie wasn't sure what to make of her sister's muted reaction. She should have been brimming with pride.

"What does that make you?" Kai asked.

Kendy's ivory smile stretched even further, pinning itself at his ears. "That makes me Wing Commander. Flynn's ready to hang it all up and ease into a comfortable retirement."

The news didn't come as a complete surprise. Flynn had seen over fifty summers. She was the oldest active dragoon by a decade. Kendy was her natural successor, and Vanna would have been the obvious pick to move up in his wake.

"About time," Effie said.

Vanna muttered Effie's name, while Kendy laughed heartily. "Effie Strait—we can always count on you to say the quiet part out loud." Vanna scowled again, but Kendy shrugged it off. "Oh, come on, Vanna. She's right, isn't she? Flying's for the young. Flynn's been over the hill since half the corps were still in nappies."

"Maybe Flynn is getting a little long in the tooth," Vanna agreed. "But she's the *last one*. The last dragoon on Volturnus who flew against the

Butcher." Kai winced at the dread pirate's mention. The name even sobered Kendy. "None of us have seen combat like that," Vanna continued. "Her experience won't be easily replaced."

"A fair point," Kendy allowed. "Flynn's been a fine Wing Commander, but she can't stay in the air forever. At some point she had to step down and let a new generation wear the patches. This piece of paper," he slammed one finger down on the letter, "says that time is now."

Vanna didn't look half so assured. Her hesitation was clearly getting to Kendy, because he quickly moved to take his leave. "I'll let you digest this information with your sister, but do try to cheer up. It's an honor, after all." He stopped at the door, backtracking with a hand over the pocket of his flight suit. "I almost forgot. Here." He tossed a bronze-wing patch of rank on the table so that it landed atop the governor's letter. "Have Effie sew it on your flight suit. The Jokai know, you're shit with a needle and thread." He bowed to Effie and Kai. "Pardon my language."

Vanna cupped a hand over the patch and watched her new commander all the way out the door.

"I'm the one who's shit with a needle and thread," Effie said.

Sliding the patch into her own pocket, Vanna changed the subject. "What kept you two so late?"

They both scrambled to answer at once, talking over each other until Kai finally deferred. "We were out at the moonberry grove. Lost track of time," Effie said.

"Is that right?" Vanna cocked an eyebrow pointedly at each of them. Effie felt the heat radiating off Kai's reddening cheeks. "Will you be staying for dinner then, Kai?"

"If you'll have me," he stammered.

They shared a spare meal of root vegetable stew and a fresh pot of tea—the previous one had boiled away. Kai ate twice as much as the girls, thanked Vanna, and took his leave.

Effie waited until she heard the door swing closed behind him before she started in again about the promotion. "What's the matter with you? This is everything you've ever wanted." *Everything short of a Leviathan,* she didn't add. Vanna had been clear that she *didn't* want to pilot a beast, even if Effie still didn't buy it.

"Effie..." Groaning, Vanna stood up from her chair and began clearing the table.

Effie snatched her own dish up and followed behind her. "I don't understand you. Why are you so afraid of your own success?"

Vanna dropped the clay bowls in her hand into the wash basin so hard that one of them cracked. "It's not *my* success that I'm afraid of, and don't be such a brat! I'm not the only one who got a letter tonight with a Celestial seal."

"So did Kendy," Effie cut in. "I already know."

"I'm not talking about Kendy!" It wasn't like Vanna to raise her voice, and the sound of it startled Effie to silence. "Flynn didn't retire, Eff. She *was* retired. Sire Ansel or Kelestina or some Patrician bean counter on Aquilon is forcing her out."

Effie shook her head. "Why would they do that?"

"I don't know." Vanna took a deep breath, her temper cooling. "But I talked to Flynn about the future of the dragoons just the other day. She seemed determined to die in her flight suit. Couldn't stand the thought of leaving her post—not after everything she's been through."

That did sound more like Flynn. Effie walked over, placed her bowl in the basin and began fishing out the shards of the broken one. "Maybe it isn't what Flynn wants," she ventured. "But what good is a Wing Commander with aching joints and a crooked spine? It doesn't serve Volturnus to let Flynn carry on like she's still twenty. It sounds like our host made a difficult decision for the good of the many."

Vanna stuck her tongue in her cheek and slouched with her hands on her hips. "The good of the many?"

"Isn't that a leader's job? To make decisions with everyone's health and safety in mind? Not just the ego of one old Elementalist."

Vanna sighed, but she didn't argue. "I don't have to like it."

"Actually, you do, Draft Lieutenant Vanna Strait."

Vanna squinted again. "You keep playing at wisdom, Eff, and they'll want you for the council of elders."

Effie snorted. "Now that's a position you can die in."

The sisters finished cleaning up together, and once the evening chores were settled, Effie returned to the table where the letter sat and ran her fingers over the calligraphy. "You will make a fine draft lieutenant, Van. Kendy better watch his back."

That earned the first honest smile from her sister that she'd seen all night.

7

EFFIE

Vanna's promotion placed her in charge of drilling the dragoon cadets. Effie and Kai took up the hobby of watching her wing train at the landing south of town, even though the activity tweaked Kai's anxiety about the tardiness of his Gift. Half the cadets were younger than they were. The newest was a twelve-year-old boy named Jaron who must've weighed eighty pounds soaking wet. His elfin features made him look more like a pet than a fellow cadet, but once the drills began, he morphed into a Jokai wind sprite, zipping across the training ground on haphazard bursts and riding untamed currents like invisible bucking pegassi.

Kai shook his head as they watched Jaron summon a gust against his back, bowling over a quartet of older cadets across the training ground like duckpins in a row.

"I'm surprised they even had a flight suit that fit him," Effie joked.

Kai didn't bite. He just watched the other cadets gusting themselves back to their feet, his handsome face drawn in an expression of wide-eyed longing that reminded Effie of the little boy he'd been just a few seasons ago.

"Eat something." She handed him a side of jerky, which he held onto but didn't eat.

"It just comes so easy for some of them," he lamented.

Effie rolled her eyes. She was starting to tire of all his hangdog moping.

Either his Gift would manifest, or it wouldn't. No amount of yearning would change that. At first, his attitude had been a mere annoyance, but the longer it persisted, the more it planted a seed of doubt in Effie's own mind. She wasn't any closer to manifesting than he was, though she'd never previously questioned whether it would happen. It was always *when*; not *if*. More than anything, she resented the way Kai forced her to face the remote possibility that she'd be the first Strait in living memory without an Elementalist Gift.

Often, she found her mind drifting back to their kiss beside the moonberry grove. He'd yet to attempt a sequel, and the way he dragged himself around the village staring at his toes, she wasn't even sure how she'd respond if he did.

Except she *was* sure. She wanted it. Dreamed of it, even. It was the one thing that might distract them both from the shrinking time before their sixteenth namedays and the Ascension Ceremony to follow.

They weren't the only ones who came to the landing to watch the dragoons. Cadet drills always attracted a crowd of enthusiastic villagers— Giftless young people doomed to a mundane life among the Volturnian plebiscite. Parents pressured their Giftless sons and daughters to court the island's dragoons on the hope that an Elementalist's contribution might thicken the family blood and yield a Gifted heir. Some Volturnian bloodlines had been without an Elementalist for generations. By decree of their host, every plebeian was equal in the eyes of the Crystal Throne, but everyone knew the unspoken pecking order. Kelestina stood at the top with her Gifted Patrician lords right beneath her. Next came the dragoons and the other Gifted. The mundane masses came last. Even among the Giftless, some bloodlines were considered thinner than others. Effie saw the ghost of this hierarchy in the fawning way the dragoon spectators behaved at the training grounds. She saw it in the colorful variety of dresses worn by Giftless young women and the boorish wrestling matches taking place between Giftless young men eager to demonstrate their worth.

It all seemed a bit pathetic to Effie. Even if she'd been born to the thinnest of Volturnian bloodlines, she'd never abase herself with such a display. She just couldn't see herself playing the role of fawning adulator, her greatest aspiration the latent Gifts of her hypothetical get.

Vanna flew in a diagonal holding pattern over the training grounds, barking orders at the awkward gaggle of half-baked Elementalists below.

"Sit on your Jokai-damned hands, Jaron! What did I tell you? If you can't control the burst, don't summon it. You want to blow yourself off the edge of the island and over bare sky? Kadir, Philia, Seulin—to me."

Three of the more advanced cadets peeled off from the group and extended stiff arms at their sides. Air currents stirred beneath them, dimpling the grass as their feet left the ground. Gradually, they rose to meet Vanna in the sky.

Before long, Kadir lost his balance and toppled back to the landing, raising performative gasps from the crowd. A spectator who looked a few years older than Effie pushed herself past her competition and helped him gently back to his feet.

Philia and Seulin ignored the distraction below, matching Vanna's altitude. They each successfully unfurled the ruffled sails from the arms of their flight suits and entered a smooth glide. The other onlookers *oo'd* and *ahh'd*, watching the three dragoons crisscross the skies above the landing. Effie thought they were laying it on a bit thick.

"That's good, Seulin," Vanna encouraged. "No bursts under wings, Philia. We've got enough wind today to make the crossing to Avernus. *See* the currents and *compel* them. Work with what the sky supplies."

Effie ignored the grounded cadets and watched the more advanced fliers carve their paths, soaring high above the ground. Vanna looked as natural as an Avian, the Jokai-blessed avatar of the East Wind itself. How old had she been when she manifested? Fourteen, was it? Maybe thirteen, even. She flew circles around her cadets, and Effie knew it was only a fraction of what she could muster.

When Vanna gave the order to set down, Philia and Seulin crashed into imprecise landings, neither one maintaining her feet. Alone in the sky, Vanna suddenly banked into a sharp climb, summoning gusts under her wings in just the manner she had cautioned against. Fists of wind gathered beneath her arms, pushing her higher and higher as she shrank against the bright blue sky. She tucked her arms and began to spin, eyes spotting a single point on the ground below. A vortex spooled around her as Vanna shot toward the ground with enough speed to shatter every bone in her body.

She didn't shatter. The wind loved Vanna. As she approached the ground, the vortex inverted to cushion her fall, tousling all the cadets around her as she landed posed on one knee. Cheers from the audience and cadets alike met her performance, while Kai moaned beside Effie. At last, he took a gloomy bite of his jerky.

Vanna wasn't showing off for the audience's benefit. Not even for her cadets, Effie realized. Sire Ansel had come down from his manse with three of his conscripted retainers. They rode in on four white mares from his household stable, imported stock from beyond the Zephyr Isles. The governor liked to train them for sport, and there were no terrestrial horses native to Volturnus. The villagers instead domesticated gold-breasted yaks and used them as beasts of burden, pulling wagons and tilling fields.

Kendy walked beside the governor, drawn away from his own drills with the active corps. He waved to Vanna, and she floated in an arc across the landing to greet Sire Ansel's retinue.

"What's he down for, you think?" Kai asked.

Effie shook her head. "I don't know, but I want to go listen."

They pushed as close as they dared, which forced them among the flouncing spectators. Effie shoved past the knitter's daughter, Ina Laurens, who huffed contemptuously at the back of Effie's head. Ina acted like the mayor of the spectators—with her perfect skin and hourglass waist. Her long, chestnut hair always fell in the perfect rippling wave. Boys seemed to like her; Effie didn't.

"Sire." Vanna bowed her purple bob, acknowledging Ansel before Kendy. "Wing Commander."

Sire Ansel dismounted his horse and handed the reins to one of his plebeian retainers. He loomed large even next to Kendy. The two men were of a similar height, but Ansel was broader around the shoulders and chest. Jeweled rings and black hair crowded his meaty hands.

"Vanna..." Kendy started, but Sire Ansel waved him silent.

"Lieutenant Strait." Ansel spoke with a high-handed accent at once foreign and imperious, as if he came from a land that had perfected the tongue ages before it ever reached Volturnus. "With everything on my desk, I wouldn't come down here without good cause, but when the Wing Commander handed me the updated lists, I had to see for myself."

Vanna glanced over at Kendy, who gave her nothing. "I'm not sure I follow, Sire."

Ignoring the implied question, Sire Ansel moved past her and scanned the landing, sizing up each of the cadet dragoons like one of his prized mares. At last, he turned back to Vanna. "How can it be that we've only added two new Elementalists to the corps since last season's Ascension?"

Vanna opened her mouth but couldn't seem to find the right words to answer the governor's question.

"As I tried to explain at the manse," Kendy cut in, stepping next to his lieutenant. "We take what the Jokai give us."

"Yes." Ansel nodded. "I've heard your explanation, Commander, but now I want to hear it from Lieutenant Strait."

Vanna just shook her head. "I—I'm not sure I have a different explanation, Sire."

"When our host arrived to deliver this island from its sorrows," he continued, "Volturnus had the most Gifted plebiscite of all the Zephyr Isles. In that first year, we discovered over two dozen Elementalists—in this village alone!"

"I'm sorry, Sire." Vanna shrugged. "What does that have to do with the price of rock on Avernus?"

"Excuse me?" Ansel frowned.

"One year has little and less to do with the next," she said. "This year, two Elementalists manifested powers strong enough to serve in the corps... so we have two new dragoons in the corps. It's as simple as that."

Ansel considered that answer for a moment, still frowning. "A troubling trend, you'd agree?"

Kendy stepped forward, shielding Vanna. "Sire, I think we can all agree that we'd like to see more—"

Ansel cut him off. "My question for you, Lieutenant, is *what are we going to do to fix it?*"

"Fix it?" Vanna shook her head like she didn't understand the question.

"Walk with me, Lieutenant." Ansel drew her away from the crowd and out of earshot as their conversation continued.

Effie didn't like the direction of this discussion—not one bit. It felt more like an interrogation. As if Vanna had any control over how many Elementalists were born on Volturnus.

"She's in over her head with this one," Effie said, but she was talking to herself. At some point, Kai had drifted away. She spotted him standing alone across the landing, seemingly dumbstruck, staring out over the open sky.

Here we go again. Another one of Kai's melodramatic moments. Sire

Ansel's line of questioning must have set him off. Effie checked Vanna and Ansel over her shoulder, then trekked off to extract him from the depths of self-pity.

She found Kai in a trance, eyes moving in chaotic patterns, darting left and right and up and down, tracking something only he could see. A mad smile accompanied this bizarre behavior. It was the first time in weeks Effie had seen his teeth.

"What's the matter with you?" She shoved his arm.

He barely moved. "Effie...I see it."

"See what?" She formed a visor with her hand and looked out beyond the edge of the landing, but the only thing she saw was empty sky.

"The *wind*." Kai spoke the word prayerfully. "It's like...lines of color—colors without names. Or *textures*, rather. I can see where they come from—where they're going. How fast and how slow! The air is so *full*... Effie... I can *see* it!" He turned to her, and suddenly he was yelling. "I can see the wind!" He flipped his head to the sky and howled like a lunatic. Cackling with laughter, Kai ran out to the edge of the landing and screamed it once more. "I can *see the wind*!"

The commotion drew everyone's attention. Effie, still frozen where he left her, watched the cadet dragoons rushing toward Kai. The pebble of self-doubt he had planted in her stomach suddenly grew to the size of a proper stone.

Vanna and Kendy left Ansel and sailed over on harnessed winds.

"That's how it starts," she heard Vanna saying. "It's like a new sense beyond sight or feeling... Almost like discovering a new color—"

"—that doesn't have a name!" Kai repeated, finishing Vanna's thought.

Vision tunneling around the three of them, Effie slowly withdrew. She should have been happy for Kai. She *was* happy for him. It was what he wanted—what he deserved. She watched Kendy slap a hand on Kai's shoulder and continued to back away.

"About time, kid," Kendy said. "We were all starting to get a little worried."

The congratulatory voices squirmed together in a garbled din as Effie hastened her escape. The cadets closed in a tight-knit circle around Vanna, Kendy and Kai. Even Sire Ansel had wandered closer, eyeing the celebration with cautious intrigue.

Effie was the only one moving in the other direction—the only one who needed to get away.

8

EFFIE

After Kai's Gift manifested, Effie stopped coming to the landing to watch the cadets at their drills. She didn't see much of Kai anymore, either. He dove headfirst into his training, desperate to hone his skill as an Elementalist.

"It's common with late bloomers," Vanna told her. "He feels like he has to catch up." Then, smiling coyly, she added, "He *is* awfully eager."

The whole thing was enough to make Effie vomit—Vanna's patronizing amusement most of all.

Kai's sixteenth nameday passed without much fanfare, then Effie's a month later to similar results. She didn't even get the day off from chores. She came home with a wheelbarrow of firewood and found Vanna sitting at the table putting the finishing touches on a cake from Kai's uncle's shop.

"Happy nameday, Eff," Vanna beamed. She hadn't even bothered to take off her flight suit. For Effie, that unintended insult was the final straw.

She declined the offered seat, groaning peevishly. "I don't suppose Kai will be joining us?"

Vanna's smile vanished. "He's working with the wing tonight on Kendy's watch. He's really coming along." Perhaps noticing her sister's mood darkening, Vanna changed tack. "He did ask me to give you this—" She fished around in her flight suit pocket and produced a hand-drawn card on a sheaf of vellum. Vellum was more difficult to come by on Volturnus than the parchment sheafs most of the villagers used for messages and record keeping. It was an expensive gesture, but Effie couldn't muster the grace to accept it.

"Just leave it on the table," she said. "I'm not hungry. I'm going to bed."

The abandoned cake, at least, gave her a bright idea. The next morning, she woke up before the sun and walked across the village square to Uncle Kellen's bakery. She needed a way to avoid all the scut work assigned by the censors while she waited for her Gift. With Kai off every waking hour with the dragoons, she imagined Uncle Kellen could use the extra pair of hands at the kiln.

Kellen was a jovial round-faced man with thinning hair and the same lean build as his nephew. An impressive feat that he maintained it, working as he did over a village's worth of bread and sweets. He welcomed her proposal with open arms and immediately set her mixing dough from a mountain of flour fresh from the mill.

It was mindless work for the most part, which left Effie too much time to worry every indignity visited upon her by her sister and Kai. At least it kept her from the fields. Part of her that she stubbornly refused to give voice hoped she and Kai might be more likely to stumble upon each other while she was working with Kellen, but Kai had moved out of the bakery after he turned sixteen, choosing to live at the corps bunkhouse with some of the other unmarried dragoons.

One stormy midwinter day, while she was mixing a batch of the next morning's dough, her unspoken wish came true. Kai burst through the front door in full dragoon regalia, hair and flight suit dripping from the rain. "Uncle Kellen—I need a baker's dozen of your sesame flatbreads for the bunkhouse. Everyone's grounded from the rain—" He stopped in his tracks as soon as he spotted Effie behind the bread counter. "What are you doing here?"

"What am I..." Effie's voice became a growl. "I work here!" How many weeks since they'd last seen each other, and that was what he had to say to her? In an instant, the dry powder of malaise and unrequited longing ignited into a rageful conflagration.

"Oh." He looked confused for a second, then started putting the pieces together. "Oh! That's great!"

Effie bared her teeth and rightly snarled at him.

"I mean it, Eff!" He put up his hands, placatingly. "I've been worried about Uncle Kellen. The bakery is a great place to work."

What about this was great? She was standing here wrist-deep in bread dough, kneading away the final months before their Ascension while he played dragoon with Vanna, flaunting the very Gift that was her birthright.

Misreading the moment entirely, he turned the conversation back to himself. "I know I haven't been around as much—"

"*As much*?" Effie forced the words through gritted teeth.

"But Vanna says I'm making great strides!"

"*Vanna says—*"

"Look!" He raised his hands and began moving them back and forth over the outline of a sphere. Effie rolled her eyes. She recognized the exercise. She'd seen Vanna replicate it a thousand times before.

At first, nothing happened, and a cruel smirk began to stretch across Effie's lips, then a few hanging bowls and baking implements began to rattle on the walls. A sphere of wind took shape between his palms, currents gathering, tightening like a ball of yarn as his hands traced the pattern. The air moved with greater and greater speed until even poor Giftless Effie could see the currents.

"Do you see it!" Earnest, tone-deaf excitement beamed from his every pore. "Vanna says it's a promising sign. Not every Elementalist is strong enough in the Gift to shape the winds like this. Most of the dragoons— they just guide the currents already in the air, you know?"

As he carried on, his hands slipped from the pattern, and Effie noticed a chink developing in the windshaped sphere. Kai's expression faltered as he struggled to regain control, but the sphere had already spun off its axis. It dispersed in a wild blast of air that shook every bowl and implement on the shelves around the bakery. The errant gust struck the pile of flour in front of Effie, frosting her from head to toe.

Momentarily blinded, she fumbled for a washrag and wiped the flour out of her eyes. She saw Kai standing open-mouthed with one of those sheepish expressions she used to find so endearing on his too-handsome face.

"E-Effie—I'm so sorry—"

"Stop." Her voice became quiet again, her rage cooling from hot ore to frozen steel.

"I can go," he stammered. "I don't need—"

"No." She threw the washrag down and undid her apron so that it pooled on the ground at her feet. "You. Stay. I'm going." She stomped across the bakery, clipping Kai with her shoulder as she passed. "Maybe you can use your Jokai-damned Gift to *clean the bloody floor*!" She growled in frustration as she slammed the door behind her.

Outside, the cold winter rain fell in sheets, but Effie's anger kept her warm. When she reached the door to her cottage, she looked down at herself, disheveled by rainfall and the tacky remnants of flour already starting to congeal. Her long hair hung soaking over her eyes. As she lifted her hands to gather it, she started cackling maniacally, head bent toward the weeping sky. She must have looked like a madwoman—the kind of person the elders used to exile to the lunatic colony on Lonely Spur. How had she gotten here? This wasn't how her life was supposed to be.

Effie Strait had been born to greatness. She was the orphan daughter of Vera and Errol, heroes of the Butcher's dreadful campaign. She was the sister of Draft Lieutenant Vanna Strait. Her grandparents had been Wing Commanders and their parents before them. She was going to visit every island in the archipelago by the power of her own Gift. She was going to bond a Leviathan and sail the skies of Ciel, discovering wonder after wonder until she fell off the end of the map.

A desolate calm came over her as she felt those dreams slipping from her rain-slicked grasp.

She had less than four months until their host delivered the list for this year's Ascension Ceremony. If she still hadn't manifested her Gift, what chance did she have to be on it? It did her no good standing out in the rain feeling sorry for herself—brought her no closer to her goals.

And she *would* reach her goals—by sheer force of will, if that was what the Jokai demanded.

She clutched her stomach, doubling over with sudden shame. Her behavior over the weeks and months since Kai joined the dragoons sickened her. How much she had hated Kai's moping back when they were both still equally Giftless—a lifetime ago, it suddenly seemed.

She hardly recognized herself anymore. This was not the behavior of Effie Strait. Effie Strait didn't mope. When she wanted something, Effie Strait didn't whine, bargain, or beg. She took it, and not even the Jokai could stop her.

Collecting herself from the momentary breakdown, she rubbed a few patches of tacky flour from her arms and wrung out her hair, now soaked from violet to dark plum. Affecting fragile composure, she walked inside the house...

...and found the last three people she wanted to see.

9

EFFIE

Voices rose up from the sitting room askance from the cottage foyer. Effie heard her sister's tired rasp and Kendy's proud baritone as well as a third voice dripping with gilt. Unwilling to hide in her own home and fed up with her pathetic irrelevance, she walked right into the middle of the conversation as if she'd been invited.

Sire Ansel and Kendy sat in a pair of hide-covered armchairs that had belonged to her parents. A kettle cooled on the small wooden table, forgotten next to three untouched mugs of tea. Vanna knelt over the fireplace across the room, prodding a fresh log to take flame.

"It's just a little unusual, Sire—" Kendy was in the middle of rhapsodizing when he noticed Effie's haunting appearance in the entryway. "Effie? Jokai fend—you look like you've been dragged from the yak stalls."

Ansel looked at her, unspeaking, with a dyspeptic set to his jaw—as if her presence in this room that her father built were some unseemly pollution. Vanna stood up from the fireplace. Her eyes widened at her sister's disheveled appearance, but something in Effie's bearing must have warned her not to pry.

Effie nodded to Kendy and curtsied to Ansel, projecting as much dignity as she could muster in her current state. "Commander. Sire. This is an unexpected call."

Ansel's Patrician gaze didn't move from Effie, though neither did he deign to acknowledge her with his accented speech.

"We were discussing an order from Aquilon," Kendy said. "Effie, if you wouldn't mind..."

"I wouldn't," she countered.

When Effie didn't move, Kendy furrowed his brow, clearly grasping for a more explicit way to kick her out of her own home.

"Why don't you stand by the fire and dry off," Vanna said, watching Ansel as she did.

Kendy rounded on her. "Vanna, it's hardly appropriate—"

"It's fine," Ansel interrupted. "The girl's clearly made up her mind, and I have a pathological affection for stubborn mares. Besides, I can hardly keep Lieutenant Strait from sharing her whereabouts with her sister."

Ignoring the intended insult, Effie lifted her skirt in another quick curtsy and scurried over by the fire next to Vanna.

Searching the awkward silence for his train of thought, Kendy stammered, "As I was saying, Sire, it's an unusual request."

"It's not a request, Commander, it's an order." Ansel's sneer could have spoiled yak's milk. "Our host has received troubling tidings from the Governor of Aeolus. A rebel faction of the plebiscite has taken up arms to deny our host her tithe. To hear their Patrician governor tell it, his manse is practically under siege."

Effie perked up with interest. The tithe was the price of the Celestials' protection from all the horrors out on the open sky—an almost holy obligation. The people of Aeolus would remember Maug's reign of terror as sharply as anyone on the isles. What could possibly possess them to deny their host her due?

"Aeolus has its own dragoon corps, Sire," Vanna said. "Shouldn't they be handling the uprising? We don't have the context."

Ansel grimaced. "The dragoons are helping the rebels." His side-eye touched Effie, as if he begrudged sharing this bit any wider than it needed to be shared. "Our host wants it handled with as little bloodshed as possible. Her Elementalists are precious to her, even if this lot's been led... astray."

Kendy sucked air through his teeth. "Are you sure there isn't some misunderstanding? If what you're saying is true, you're asking us to pit Zephyri against Zephyri. Dragoon against dragoon."

"If what Sire Ansel says is true," Effie blurted out, "then the rebels are no true Zephyri. Anyone who takes up arms against our host or her Patrician governor is a traitor to their home and island."

She locked eyes with Ansel and tapped into some hidden well of defiance unleashed by all the recent indignities she suffered. The defiance buttressed her to stand in his judgmental silence without blinking until he finally rewarded her with a slight, black-headed nod. "I quite agree." He turned to Kendy. "As our host's chosen Wing Commander, I'm sure you share the girl's worthy sentiments?"

It was the first time Effie had ever seen Kendy at a loss for words. She felt Vanna's hand guiding her to the periphery as her sister stepped forward. "I don't know about this, Sire. I've never heard of the Volturnus Dragoons being deployed in such a way. Can't our host send a ship from the Armada? Our fliers won't like the idea of crossing wings with other dragoons."

"Maybe you won't have to," Effie said.

"Effie—" Vanna sounded exasperated.

"No—" Sire Ansel cut in. "I'd hear what the girl has to say. She seems to be the only one here with enough moral clarity to meet the moment."

For a tense beat, Effie thought her sister might object, but Vanna stepped aside and yielded the floor.

Effie seized her moment, even though her sister's disapproval burned like the sun on her back. "The Armada is full of warships and trained soldiers," she reasoned. "The only tool available to them is force. Sire Ansel said that our host values her Elementalists. She's sending the Volturnus Dragoons because she wants this handled quietly. Commander, you run joint exercises with the Aeolus Dragoons every summer. You know these fliers. Go hear their grievances and see if you can't make them stand down without a fight. It's the only chance to de-escalate."

"From the mouths of babes." Ansel nodded again and lifted his hand in mock toast before pointing at Kendy and Vanna. "You two need to muster a detachment from your wing—only the strongest fliers. You leave as soon as this storm breaks. I understand a fully-fledged dragoon can make the crossing unaided in less than a day."

Kendy and Vanna shared a meaningful look. "As our host commands," Kendy answered.

"Grand." Ansel checked the timepiece on his wrist and stood up, patting his own satin-legged thighs. Kendy scrambled to find his feet, as well.

"You have your orders, and I should be going," the governor said. "My staff will be around with my coach any minute, and it wouldn't be courtly to leave them standing in the rain." He nodded to each of them as he moved for the exit. "Commander. Lieutenant." His gaze lingered for a moment on Effie. "I apologize—I don't think I caught your name."

"Effie Strait," Effie said, lifting her tattered skirt for one final curtsy, deeper than all the rest.

Ansel answered the gesture with a stiff bow. "Good evening, Effie Strait."

10

VANNA

The rainstorm broke with the dawn.

Vanna and Kendy argued over which fliers to tap for the crossing. He wanted to pluck Seulin and Jaffe from the bunkhouse, but Vanna wouldn't have it.

"They aren't ready."

"Says you," Kendy countered. "Seulin's as Gifted as half the active corps."

"Gifted, yes," Vanna agreed. "But she's still a cadet, and that means I decide when she's ready to go."

Not wishing to argue, Kendy deferred, as Vanna knew he would. He was a commander with many fine qualities but in an argument, her sheer stubbornness always won the day.

"What about Kai?" he asked.

Vanna scoffed.

"What?"

"Don't be ridiculous."

"He's sixteen and as dedicated a cadet as I've ever seen. He's already windshaping. He reminds me of you."

"We're not even discussing this."

Kendy put too much stock in the Gift. Training and experience were worth at least as much, and if this turned into a combat situation, they'd be worth a great deal more. Kai *would* be a valuable flier, but with fewer than six months training in the cadet corps he was still too raw.

In the end, they called up eight of the full dragoons, six windshapers and two gliders with weaker Gifts but over ten years in a flight suit. Senna, Raji, Prestor and Kale were the four strongest fliers after Vanna and Kendy. Dray had been Kendy's bunkmate when they were both young cadets, and even though Kendy quickly outstripped him in ability, their new commander still trusted the muscular flier to hold his wing. Lya was the same age as Kai, but she'd manifested early and spent two years drilling with the corps before Kendy finally gave her her wings. Her brother Jin was two years older and too weak in the Gift to windshape, but he made up for that weakness with dedication and aerial poise. Vanna trusted him as much on a long crossing as any stronger Elementalist. Hal was the last flier selected, a forty-year-old veteran with twenty years of service in the corps. Rumor had it he was Flynn's preferred choice for Draft Lieutenant until Kendy made himself inevitable. If Hal chafed under such young leadership, he never once let it show.

The ten dragoons assembled outside the bunkhouse and made the two-hour hike together to the windward launch outside of town. Kendy divided them into two drafts, one for Vanna to lead and one for himself. Once the group had nearly claimed the launch, he dropped a black duffle bag at his feet and distributed flight extensions to a chorus of aggravated moans.

"None of that," Kendy barked. "We're making a straight crossing to Aeolus Isle, and I won't have you tiring over open sky."

The wooden chassis of the extensions clipped onto the back of a dragoon flight suit and deployed two billowing canvas sails. They looked like kite-ship masts rendered in miniature, and every dragoon hated them. The cruciform supports were uncomfortable for anyone under six-feet tall and cumbersome in the air. Improved efficiency over a long crossing came at the cost of maneuverability. For the more acrobatic Elementalists in the corps, this was a bitter tradeoff. Like any tool, Vanna supposed they had their place, and this kind of straight crossing was certainly it, but if it turned into a dogfight as they approached Aeolus, she was ready to let her draft abandon them.

Kendy helped her with her clips before she turned to do the same for her draft. Senna grumbled the loudest about it. She stood a mere hair over five feet, so the extension fit awkwardly, its weight a nuisance that would hamper her elite speed.

"Just over bare sky," Vanna whispered. "You can ditch it once we reach Aeolian airspace."

This seemed to calm her some.

Two silhouettes—one portly; one thin—awaited them at the launch, hovering beside a commandeered gatherer's cart pulled by two golden yaks.

Kendy's gaze narrowed as he prepared to gust himself up to greet them. "What's she doing here?"

"You didn't invite her?" Vanna asked.

"Why would I invite her? I only asked Bolo for a forecast." Extending his arms behind him, Kendy soared to the top of the launch, and Vanna followed.

Bolo waved from his perch against the yak cart as the two dragoon officers landed upright before him. Flynn's thin frame lurked a few feet away near the lip of the launch, her arms crossed in front of her chest as she gazed longingly at the western sky.

Kendy ignored her, moving straight for Bolo, so Vanna took it upon herself to greet their former commander. "Flynn!"

Flynn unclasped her arms to receive Vanna's embrace. She still wore her silver hair in one long braid down her back. The strength of her hug spoke to the vitality of a much younger woman.

"It's good to see you, Vanna." She didn't sound happy. "You want to tell me what the hell is going on up here?"

Vanna glanced back at Kendy before answering. "Orders from Aquilon."

"Is that right?"

She saw Kendy patting Bolo on the shoulder before gusting himself over to join her. "What are you doing here, Flynn?"

She answered with a contemptuous snort. "I was waiting out the storm with Bolo when he got your summons. Figured I'd better see what all the fuss was about before you went and got my fliers killed."

"They're not your fliers anymore," Kendy said.

"And who's fault is that?" Flynn shot back.

The rest of the dragoons in their wing claimed the promontory. The younger fliers huddled around the launch awaiting Kendy, while Hal walked up to join the conversation with Flynn.

"Ahoy, Commander," he said.

"Hal." The sight of him seemed to break some of the tension in Flynn. She sighed, flipping her silver braid over one shoulder. "I'm not here to clip your wings, Kendy. Just thought I might offer some advice." She looked over the team they'd assembled. "Not a one of you has seen real combat before."

"We don't have time, Flynn," Kendy said. "We need to make the crossing to Aeolus."

Flynn's eyes flared wide and white. "What's on Aeolus?"

Kendy shook his head dismissively. "I'm going to get Bolo's forecast. Vanna, make sure your draft is ready for launch."

Vanna tapped out a salute with one hand over the bronze wing of rank on her flight suit. "Aye, Commander."

Flynn stared daggers at the back of Kendy's head as he soared off. "It should be me leading this mission," she grumbled. "That boy's going to get someone killed."

"Don't be sore on him, Commander." Hal scratched his thinning head. "Kendy's a fine Wing Commander. Learned from the best, didn't he?"

Flynn only grunted.

"I'd hear that advice, if you're still offering," Vanna said.

Flynn's expression looked pained—as if she suspected she was being patronized. She must've decided it didn't matter even if she was. "Take small formations," she started.

"We're already divided into two drafts of five."

Flynn nodded. "Lose the extensions if bullets start flying. You're just giving your enemies a bigger target."

The dragoons all fought with steel. A dragoon in flight was too nimble a target, and the clash of Gift-pressured air currents made the shooting trajectories impossible to judge. Vanna herself wore one rapier at her back and two short daggers on her hips. It was all the blade anyone needed over open sky. Of course, Flynn didn't know they might be fighting other dragoons.

"Anything else?" Vanna asked, clocking Kendy and the rest of the dragoons standing around old Bolo to get the forecast.

"Only a thousand things!" She crossed her arms again. "But seeing as *Commander Kendy's* in a hurry, let me leave you with this: every pitched battle I ever fought was won and lost in the positioning. Whoever gets to choose the terms of engagement gets to fly away from it. You're a flight instructor now. Remember your earliest lessons. In the open air, it takes more work to go up than down. If you have the advantage of altitude, don't give it up until you're ready to strike."

"That's good advice," Hal said.

Vanna agreed. She thanked Flynn for coming even if Kendy wouldn't, then she and Hal gusted over to join the other dragoons.

Calling Bolo out to the launch was a fine idea on Kendy's part. Vanna wasn't sure she would have thought of it. The heavyset farmer had an unusual Gift for a Volturnian Elementalist. He didn't see the wind or speak to it—couldn't guide the currents or shape a gust. The Jokai had instead Gifted Bolo with stormsight. In his mind's eye, Bolo saw the weather for a thousand leagues around, and he was practiced enough to predict its changeable demeanor with prophetic accuracy up to seven days out.

By the time Vanna joined the gathering, Bolo had already entered a fugue state, drawing inward as he communed with his rare Gift. He stared off into infinity, through the open sky and the clouds above, into the dark firmament beyond. His eyes tipped back into his head, flashing an unsettling pair of red-rimmed sclera. When he returned from his fugue, he rubbed his temples and offered Kendy a confident nod.

"The storm's east of us now," he said. "It's still drizzling over the moonflow, but most of what's left of her's out over open sky." He pointed to the dim shape of their neighboring island. "A few pockets of moisture forming over Avernus, but they'll all blow themselves out before they get a chance to organize. You'll hit one patch of rough sky between here and Aelous, but it's nothing you dragoons can't handle." Bolo formed an L with his thumb and forefinger and moved the bracket ninety degrees—from the outline of distant Avernus to the red crescent of the rising sun. "Only thing to worry about is a few squall lines moving toward the windward shore of Aeolus. They're going to batter the island in about three days before pushing north-north-east off the lees and into Spurrian airspace."

"We'll be long gone by then," Kendy said.

"See that you are."

"Thank you, Bolo." Their commander saw the Gifted forecaster up into his yak cart and sent both him and a sour-faced Flynn on their way back to the village.

"Senna, Raji, Prestor, and Hal on Vanna," Kendy said. "Dray, Kale, Lya, and Jin with me."

Vanna collected her draft, performing one final weapons check on each of them before inspecting their extensions. She ran bare fingers over each canvas sail in search of weak spots and holes. Finding none, she signaled the all-clear to Kendy. Their Wing Commander claimed the edge of the launch, raised both fists over his head then dropped them, signing liftoff.

Vanna stepped into his draft and spoke to the wind.

Its mischievous voice played in her ears—clear as the midday bell ringing out from the village campanile. She gathered two gusts beneath her wings and shot out into the open blue.

The sun had nearly crested the horizon. Its golden orb cast a halcyon glow over the empty vastness before her. Eddies in the air currents whispered the positions of each flier in her draft as they fell into a formation V. Vanna extended one open palm over her head—the air-sign to claim altitude. She drew fists of wind beneath her, forcing them against her canvas sails.

The Volturnus Dragoons began to climb.

11

VANNA

Vanna drove her formation along a sharp angle of ascent until they burst through a layer of clouds. Once the altimeter on her flight suit indicated 500 feet above the meridian, she leveled out, steadying as her draft fell in line along her wings. The winter air bit at such great heights, its icy claws finding every seam in her insulated flight suit. Frigid sky was the price of making such a hurried crossing. Not even Vanna had the strength to force a gust beneath her wings for half-a-day's flying—not without exhausting herself in the process.

The clouds thinned as they entered Avernian airspace, passing just south of the island's leeward tip where the scarred site of the Old Village glared up at them through the open sky. From her birds-eye view, Vanna tracked the outlines of broken homes, walls reduced to rubble; thatched roofs all but blasted away. Bald scars pockmarked the land where nature struggled to reassert itself—a memento of Maug the Butcher's violent assault. Aeolus and Avernus saw the worst of Devil Ray's bombardment. They endured days of cannon fire and burning alchemical rain, driving every last survivor out of their settlements, seeking succor beneath the jungle canopy's meager shield. Vanna was only four years old during Maug's reign of terror. She remembered following her mother out to Volturnus' windward launch where they watched the explosions erupt over neighboring Avernus. Devil Ray's black silhouette revealed itself with each artillery report, a wraith lit by sheets of lightning, the thunder of cannon fire presaging each strike.

After the Celestials drove Maug away, the Aeolians elected to rebuild, but it proved too painful for the people of Avernus to return to their Old Village in the lees. They picked a new site for their settlement and, with help from their Patrician governor, began construction from scratch. The remains of the Old Village they left as a reminder of all they had lost—all they might lose again without their host's protection.

Avernus receded behind Vanna's formation as she entered the meditative state of open flight. With nothing to look at in the bare sky below and the natural winds pushing her sails, her thoughts turned to Effie.

Her sister had seemed rudderless these many months, drowning under the weight of each passing day without her Gift. For months now, she'd feared her sister might never manifest—might not be the Elementalist they all assumed she'd eventually become. These fears had only grown since the passing of Effie's sixteenth nameday, though Vanna hadn't yet dared to give them voice. How surprised she was when Effie, dripping with rainwater and youthful pride, forced her way into the meeting with Sire Ansel and insisted on speaking out of turn. She told the Patrician governor exactly what he wanted to hear, and if the interference rankled Vanna, the nagging part of her that worried over Effie's diminished spirits had been somewhat balmed by the bold display. Her sister had stolen command of the discussion from two dragoon officers and a Patrician lord. She'd shown more fire than Vanna had seen from the girl in a month of Moondays. She'd seemed like *Effie* again—instead of the self-pitying changeling that replaced her. Her sister had never been one to accept defeat with a white flag of surrender. Even if she wasn't Gifted—even if the Ascension Ceremony came and went without her name making the lists—Effie would persevere.

The dragoons crossed out of Avernian airspace around midday and into the skies surrounding Aeolus. Kendy's draft climbed into view. He banked his formation toward Vanna, signaling descent with two extended palms. Vanna passed the command to her draft formation and banked into a shallow dive.

She sighted a small skerry a few degrees off her angle of descent and adjusted to follow Kendy's formation into a landing. The wings of her extension retracted as Vanna tucked her legs into a standing stop, pulling headwinds through the Gift to slow her final approach. Her formation followed, with only Prestor stumbling into an awkward heap upon contact with the land. Shaking her head, Senna went to help the blushing dragoon back to his feet.

Small, uninhabited islands lay scattered around the skies of the Zephyr Archipelago. This particular skerry surfaced at an unusually high altitude—almost 300 feet above the meridian, according to Vanna's altimeter. It was the sort of island that was easy to miss, which made it a fine landing for smugglers and pirates to exploit.

Some ragged brush off to the windward side of the skerry provided a home for a family of skygulls, but these were the rocky island's only native life. If she squinted hard enough, Vanna could see all the way across the skerry, from one edge to the next.

"What are we doing here?" Stretching her stiff arms, Vanna walked up to Kendy. "We need to keep going. We're less than fifty leagues from the shore of Aeolus."

"Saw something from the air," Kendy said. "Something big. Dragoons, on me."

Vanna waved her draft, all of whom were still stretching and gathering themselves up from the long crossing. They followed Kendy down a small embankment on the windward side of the skerry, sliding down on loose gravel until they came upon two abandoned kite-ships moored in the embankment's shadow—the only spot on the bare island that afforded any cover.

Kendy and Vanna exchanged a meaningful look and gusted over to inspect.

The ships were both of the same make, with four symmetrical sails—two bottom spinnakers mounted from the keel and two furled-up square sails tied to the mainmast. The ships' bellows connected to a pedal system inside the cockpit. Kendy worked his way around the nearest ship until he reached the stern where a set of twin propellers sat above the rudder. The dragoon commander stuck his hand inside the casing and spun the turbines.

They certainly weren't wrecks. To Vanna's trained eye, both ships looked to be in fine flying condition, and whoever left them here had taken the time to furl the sails and stake the moorings.

"Smugglers?" Vanna suggested.

"Maybe..." Kendy continued tinkering with the propeller. "Smugglers usually use the skerries to hide caches of goods, though—not a pair of outland kite-ships. Look here—" Vanna came around to face the propellers. "That's an intake line from a steam engine. The shipyards on Aeolus don't make them like this. I've never seen its like from Grenport, either."

"Uh, Commander—" Hal's voice rose up from the other side of the ships. "I think you'll want to get a look at this."

Vanna and Kendy exchanged an ominous look before gusting over to see what Hal had discovered. He and Jin dragged two canvas duffels camou-flaged to look like the rocky ground out from a hidden cache beneath a mound of gravel. They dumped them both out and leapt back, startled by the contents.

Guns. More guns than Vanna had ever seen—enough to arm a small militia. Three-dozen flintlock hand cannons and flamework rifles with long-toothed bayonets. Among the smaller guns, a ground-based sail-cutter lay disassembled next to its mount and a case of discus shells.

The ten dragoons gathered in a circle around the pile of artillery. Vanna knelt down to pick up one of the sail-cutter shells.

"Looks like Armada tech," she said.

"You think the Armada left these weapons here?" Kendy sounded skeptical.

Vanna *didn't* think so, but if the cache didn't belong to the Celestials, only one other explanation served, and she liked that one even less.

"Put these back where you found them," Kendy told Hal. "Prepare to launch for Aeolus."

Vanna followed him up the hill as Hal and the other dragoons gathered the weapons back into their duffels. "You're just going to leave them there?"

"What would you have me do, Vanna?"

"Throw them over the side of the island!"

"And let whoever left them know we found them out? Outland kite-ships. Flintlock pistols. We both know what this means."

She did. Pirates, and not the petty crews likely to be frightened off by a wing of dragoon fliers.

"I won't risk drawing unwanted attention to the islands," Kendy said. "Let's hope they're passing through."

They crested the hill together and began to assemble for launch. "Doesn't it seem a little coincidental to you?" Vanna asked. "We find a pirate cache on a skerry while we're on our way to put down an uprising on Aeolus?"

"What are you saying, Vanna? You think there are pirates among the rebels on Aeolus?" He pivoted to the approaching dragoons. "Draft on me." Vanna paused before calling her own draft to attend her. The intensity of her gaze lured Kendy's attention back her way. "What is it, Lieutenant?"

"We don't know what we're flying into on Aeolus."

Kendy set his strong jaw and prepared to lift off. "We have our orders. Keep your formation loose."

Vanna's draft spread from formation V into the flying chevron. They followed Kendy's draft from a higher altitude, watching his grouping as the leeward coast of Aelous came into view below. Kendy's wing banked into their initial approach. Without scouting reports from the island proper, Kendy meant to set them down on the farthest landing, several leagues south of the village. They'd make their final approach over land, with fleet-footed Senna ranging ahead to provide scouting reports.

Vanna spotted the landing just as the skies erupted with a concussive sound that filled her mind with images she wished she could forget.

"Cannon!" Kendy's voice sounded very distant, thinned by the howling winds.

Another round of blasts. Vanna was suddenly four years old again, standing on the edge of Volturnus watching the world end for the defense-less Avernians across the gulf.

"Cannon!" She heard herself repeating, screaming as loud as her voice permitted, praying it would be enough for the fliers at the tips of her chevron to hear.

Vortices whined at her through the Gift, their lines of force converging, trailing each projectile as it streaked through the sky. Heavy iron cannon-balls screamed past her draft, finding holes in her formation by nothing short of flier's luck.

Gathering her wits in an instant, Vanna gave the open-armed air-sign to disperse and pursue an evasive landing. Kendy's draft had already scattered. The wing commander climbed to Vanna's altitude as his fliers shot for the landing below without their lead. Vanna felt the winds bending toward Kendy, spiraling around him as he claimed a near-vertical ascent.

He pulled up next to Vanna, and she used her own Gift to match his speed, flying close enough to reach out and touch his wings.

"My draft will take the windward descent," Kendy said. "Send your fliers on the lees. We divide their fire and get these dragoons on the ground."

Vanna saluted with one fist against her chest as Kendy peeled off to hold the rear. He wouldn't land until he knew each of his fliers touched down safely on Aeolus—no less than she'd expect from her wing commander.

The crackle of cannon fire rang out once more from the island below. Five more explosions followed by five more projectiles hurtling toward their wing. This time, the assailants on Aeolus had trained their fire on Kendy's descending draft, but the dragoons had already pivoted for their windward approach. Vanna watched from altitude as each misfired cannonball passed harmlessly through their wake.

The cannoneers needed time between each report to reload. Vanna seized her window and signaled her swarming fliers to take the leeward descent. They were still a few miles off the Aeolian shore, and that position prevented her from following the sharp angle she would have preferred. Good sense dictated an evasive trajectory, but Vanna couldn't stand the delay. The shortest path was a perfect geodesic, and that was what she followed, desperate to lead her dragoons to solid ground. Vanna flared the gusts beneath her wings with all the power in her Gift. If they were just fast enough, they could set down on the landing before the cannons' next report.

The solid ground of Aeolus rose up to meet her at a breakneck pace. Vanna dove, knifing through the skies like a human projectile, racing against the reload time of the cannons. Her ears popped, cheeks screaming with friction. She tucked her legs beneath her and, with a triumphant shout, touched solid ground and skidded to a stop on the landing.

The rest of Kendy's draft had already made landfall, but they didn't look like they shared her relief. They hardly even reacted to her arrival, eyes still fixated on the Aeolian skies beyond.

Panic returned as Vanna realized what she'd done.

She whipped around to see the dragoons in her draft still sailing through open sky, their movements impossibly slow. She'd left them more than a league behind her, unable to keep pace with her plunging descent.

Too fast. She'd been too fast. Vanna was stronger in the Gift than anyone on Volturnus. Stronger, even, than Kendy. In her frantic haste to make landfall, she'd left all her people behind, hanging exposed in the Aeolian sky. The sound of the cannons knocked all the air from her lungs. She watched in horror as five projectiles careened toward her dragoons— the four fliers left under her command, *under her care.*

Senna, Raji, Prestor, and Hal all sped toward the cannon fire, driving inside the weapons' critical range, following the same exposed path described by Vanna. Senna was quick enough to fall into an evasive trajectory—and Raji and Prestor each found safe sky by the grace of whatever Jokai protected them—but Hal was not so lucky. Vanna cried out as the cannonball ripped through the sail of his extension, knocking the veteran dragoon into a spinning, uncontrolled descent.

No. Vanna prayed for Hal to find his bearings, to use his Gift to right himself, but Hal was no windshaper. He'd entered freefall, and for him there would be no escape. Kendy was too far above and behind to do anything but watch impotently as his dragoon began the Long Drop through bare sky.

Drawing deep from the Elementalist well of her Gift, Vanna jettisoned her extension and blasted herself back into the sky. She ignored all the swirling currents around her, relying only on the wind she shaped, driving every line of force beneath the ruffles of her flight suit. Unencumbered by the extension, she cut through the sky with surgical precision, eyes locked on the chaotic freefall of her wounded dragoon.

For one petrifying second, Vanna knew with certainty that she would not make it. The friction of her torrid ascent warmed her insulated flight suit, but she knew it would not be enough. Screaming through gritted teeth, she pushed with every last ounce of her Gift, sure she'd erupt into a ball of fire at any moment.

She extended her arms in one desperate stretch. Hal's falling body struck her with force. They both began to tumble together, limbs tangled, the shattered wing of Hal's extension billowing uselessly in the turbulent air. Vanna maintained her grip on the unconscious flier. They continued their tumbling freefall for another hundred feet before she managed to grasp the chaotic currents to straighten their descent. Without an inch of altitude to spare, she gusted them back on a leeward approach and set down on the Aeolian landing, muscles screaming, lungs pleading for air.

Vanna rolled onto her back, panting, as the safely landed dragoons came around to administer care to the wounded flier. Some seconds later, Kendy landed and sped past Vanna, leaping to Hal's side. Raji was the first to come over and offer a skin of water, which she initially declined.

"That was incredible," he said. "You saved his life."

"After almost throwing it away," Vanna said breathlessly. Her lungs still fought to get enough air up to her throbbing head. She sat up and accepted Raji's waterskin. As she drank, Kendy left Hal's side and came over to join them. He extended his hand and pulled Vanna to her feet.

"Arm's good and broken," Kendy said. "But he'll live. Prestor set it and the pain brought him around."

"Kendy—I don't know why—"

He held up a hand to stop her. From his position at the rear of their formation, he would have had a view of the whole debacle—would have seen Vanna abandon her draft as she gusted herself to a speed no dragoon could match. "You saved him. That's all anyone will remember."

Vanna doubted that.

"Can he walk?" she asked.

"He'll have to." Kendy turned his gaze north from the landing. "Those cannons can't be far off. Let's make sure Hal's the last dragoon they ever shoot at."

12

EFFIE

Effie dreamed of Leviathan. She dreamed of sleek-bodied dauphine splashing through the moonflow and creatures so exotic she might have invented them in her unconscious mind. Eight-flippered tortoises with opalescent shells. Marble stallions the height of grain silos with six legs, eyes like burning coal, and dancing manes of wildfire. She rode one of these spectral stallions—Sleipnir—and how could she possibly know that name? The air tasted of ozone and ash as she looked out from her perch on its obsidian saddle-deck, laying eyes upon the pink sand of an approaching shoreline. Such a wonder existed nowhere in the Zephyrs—nowhere she'd ever seen. She drove Sleipnir down from its impossible altitude, hurtling through walls of wind shear on a collision path with that blushing shore.

She woke before touching down.

Vanna and the other dragoons were long gone. Her sister hadn't said anything and hadn't left a note. She might have been salty over Effie's behavior—at her mouthy display in front of Sire Ansel. Effie hadn't intended to anger her sister—certainly not before such a dangerous flight— but neither did she care that it happened. She found it difficult to muster one ounce of regret over what had been an exceptional performance on her part. She'd spoken with *moral clarity*, Sire Ansel had said. Vanna and Kendy should have thanked her for saving them from the embarrassment of their own mealy-mouthed report. She wouldn't hold her breath waiting for that gratitude, however. Most importantly of all, she'd made an impression on Sire Ansel. The governor asked for her name, and Effie suspected he'd remember it. That was the first step to making it onto his list for the Ascension.

She washed her mouth and hair in the basin and dried her violet locks between two lilac-scented towels. Instead of dressing for work in the bakery, she pulled a fresh knee-length dress from her closet and set out to find Kai. With Vanna and Kendy off Volturnus, the dragoons would be left to their own devices.

She found the bunkhouse nearly empty. Seulin was the only late riser present, still turning down her bed.

"He went to his uncle's shop," Seulin said. "Something about *owing him* for last night."

Effie thanked her for the intel and turned back the way she came.

She found Kai in the spot she'd occupied just the night before, bent over a mound of flour, practiced hands mixing the milled grain methodically into dough. Sweat stains pooled around his collar and at his armpits, and his apron hung sloppily from his chest, one back-strap dangling undone.

The bakery itself was all back in array after his disastrous windshaping display. She figured he'd spent the morning cleaning up. Seeing him without his flight suit on, working his old task next to his uncle's kiln—it filled Effie with unexpected longing. This was how the Jokai intended life to be. If only one of them could have been Gifted, by all rights, it should have been *her*. Kai was her awkward sidekick, content to work a mundane job while she met with Patrician lords and sent dragoon wings flying across the archipelago. How had they fallen so far off course? She searched his strong jaw and handsome features for that undersized boy who idolized her.

For so long, Kai only existed in her shadow, and some part of her couldn't help but feel robbed—as if he'd sponged up the Gift the Jokai intended for her. This was not how the story was supposed to go. In every telling, he grew up handsome, but hardly aware of it. He woke up every morning to bless the Jokai that Effie Strait still gave him the time of day and, when the mood moved her, allowed him a kiss.

Maybe it wasn't fair to hold Kai in that supporting role, but wasn't that exactly what he'd done to her? Fates reversed, she'd have made more time for him. Effie could almost taste that forgotten life as she watched him sifting flour into the mixing bowl, strong shoulders working as he beat the mixture into dough. In that moment, she nearly believed she could force the threads of fate back into a desirable pattern by wish and will alone.

"Effie." Kai set aside his mixing spoon and looked up with a lopsided grin that nearly undid her. For all his Gifts, he was still that boy she remembered. She hardly needed Elementalist powers to set him back in his place.

"I'm surprised to find you here," she lied. "Don't you have training?"

"No," Kai moaned. "Not today. Everyone's grounded—at least everyone who got *left behind*." A note of bitterness entered his tone as he picked up the spoon and resumed his mixing. "Vanna and Kendy took a wing out on some secret mission. Didn't tell anyone in the bunkhouse a damn thing."

"Oh." Effie twirled one purple lock of hair. She'd dried it in just such a way to hold a wave she knew he liked.

Kai looked up at her over his bowl. "Oh?"

"It's just—I might know something about that."

Kai dropped his mixing spoon again and looked at her. "What do you mean? Vanna told you where she was going?"

"Heard it myself from Sire Ansel," Effie said. "We had a meeting last night."

"Why would he meet with you?"

Effie bit down on her lip. Kai hadn't meant anything by the question, but the earnest disbelief in his tone still chafed. "Maybe he needed insight from someone with *moral clarity* to help him decide how to handle the rebellion on Aeolus."

"What?" Kai's expression nearly leapt off his face.

"Leave that," Effie said, indicating the flour and mixing bowl. "Walk with me out to the landing and I'll explain."

She recounted the conversation with Sire Ansel as promised, and if she embellished her own role in the discussion, she did so slightly and with dramatic interests in mind. By the time they were out at the landing where the dragoons trained, she had Kai hanging on her every word.

When she finished speaking, he drew on his Gift. Effie felt the winds coursing over his hands—so powerful they tousled her hair. "I should be out there with them," he lamented.

"You?" Effie laughed, and the pettiest part of her hoped the sound of it made Kai feel small. "You're just a cadet. You're not ready to make a crossing like that—let alone a landing under fire."

"You think they'd fire on dragoons?"

Effie shook her head. "I don't know. I don't know anything about these rebels besides what I told you. If it is a pirate crew out there causing trouble, though, we can't rule out the possibility it'll turn into a fight."

He nodded thoughtfully, clearly working those details over in his mind. Effie watched him, and the sense of longing returned with such depth that it threatened to swallow her whole. For the first time in a long time, the two of them stood on even footing—neither one worthy of the flight to Aeolus. Both had been left behind.

A cool winter breeze blew across the Volturnian landing, a stirring of cardinal forces in the deep sky—each wind a vector connecting Volturnus to Avernus and Aeolus far beyond. The wind rushed beneath Effie's open skirt, tickling the backs of her bare knees and raising gooseflesh to dimple her smooth legs. Embracing the chill, she left Kai standing and walked across the barren ground of the landing, beaten to submission by generations of aircraft and countless dragoons.

She walked until she reached the shore of Volturnus.

Beyond this line, her island's substance fell away, yielding as all islands did to the oblivion of Ciel's infinite sky. Feeling defiant, Effie kicked off her shoes and wriggled each painted toe. She edged toward the shore, extending her toes then the balls of her feet over open sky, desperate for one small part of her to defy the land to which she'd been bound.

She could jump if she dared it. In one of her favorite Zephyri folktales, a group of five Giftless girls on the eve of their shared sixteenth nameday threw themselves off Widow's Peak, the highest windward plateau on Volturnus. They hoped to trigger an awakening of their latent Gifts, so assured such powers were their due. For one girl among them, the gambit worked, while the rest fell into infinity. To fall over bare sky—it was the worst fate on the face of Ciel. The Long Drop.

It was a cautionary story, as so many folktales tended to be. But in this moment, Effie drew from it some reckless inspiration. If she gathered four more Giftless girls to join her in this drop, would she not be the one to rise?

"Effie..." Kai had crept up behind her without her noticing him.

"This is the place where your Gift manifested," she said, still watching the empty sky. Even without looking, she could sense he stood but an arm's length away—close enough to catch her if she tried anything rash.

"It is," he said.

"What did it feel like?"

Kai's breathing banished the howl of the winds, overpowered the distant flock of gulls trading shrill complaints. "It felt like opening a third eye," he said, and she could sense him edging closer. "It felt like hearing colors or tasting sounds."

"I don't hear any colors," Effie confessed. Kai's strong hands found her shoulders. Once baker's iron, those hands had been wrought like steel in a monger's forge—tempered by endless hours training on these very grounds.

She let her weight press against him, away from the shore over which her toes still dangled. As she felt the pressure between them building, a gust of wind encircled the two of them, coursing in unnatural spirals that bound their being into one. The winds held fast around them, ruffling the edges of Effie's skirt, billowing her scented hair so that the impression of lilacs overwhelmed them. It was a shaped wind—and she could not see it. She could not taste its name nor hear its scent.

"That's what it feels like," Kai said, not realizing the damning confirmation he offered.

Effie squinted back tears welling in her eyes and silently cursed their betrayal. Effie Strait didn't cry over defeat. Effie Strait knew nothing of futility. Effie Strait was many things and more...

But she wasn't an Elementalist.

Choking back the sobs building in her throat, she turned to face Kai. She searched the brown pools of his eyes for some hint of remorse, some fleck of shame over the way he had left her. She found none of it, and though she expected to be repulsed by the pity in its place, she found no such rocks to break against. Kai's guileless eyes surprised her for once. In their brown depths, she saw only a deep and abiding sadness. Rage, even, that he had not the power to spare her this Giftless fate. She could have kissed him.

So she did.

Effie stood up on her toes and pressed her lips against his. The moment was so unlike that first kiss beneath the moonberry grove. He felt rougher than before, chapped by the winds of flight. Kai didn't pull away, but neither did he purse his lips to meet hers. His own mouth never parted, never let her inside to test the flavor of his tongue. And when she was finished, he did not hold her.

Despondent, Effie fell back to the flats of her feet. She would not look away. Standing her ground seemed the only way to grasp some tattered remnant of her dignity—to shield against such abject exposure.

Kai backed away from her. "I'm sorry, Eff," he stammered.

"Don't." Her voice felt lifeless—emptied of all its song. She'd give this boy no more tears. He'd taken enough from her as it was. "Don't apologize to me."

"It's just the training—"

"Stop it!" Her raised voice made him flinch, providing just enough satisfaction for Effie to hold onto. "Go back to your training, then." His lips moved wordlessly, but he was already backing away. He *wanted* to be away. "Go!" she shouted after him.

Bowing his head in surrender, Kai turned and drew upon his Gift to hasten his escape.

She watched him glide across the landing on stolen wind.

The least of what he'd stolen that day.

13

VANNA

Kendy sent Senna out ahead to scout. She returned to the landing within the hour, a smug look on her elfin face.

"They're exposed," she said with confidence. "Heavy cannons set up less than a league north of here. They're on a hilltop overlooking the leeward shore—cannon position backs up against the jungle's edge."

"How many?" Kendy asked.

Senna held up an open palm—*five*. "Didn't see any sidearms. I don't think they were expecting a ground invasion. The site's set up for air defense."

"Good. Shouldn't take more than eight of us to disarm them. We'll cut through the jungle, approach from the west."

Vanna listened to Kendy detail their plan of attack. Hal was in no condition to fly, so he and Prestor went ahead to scout the village while the rest of them sailed across the jungle and struck from the treetops.

Free of their flight extensions, the Volturnian dragoons moved with alacrity, skirting over the jungle canopy with Vanna at the leading edge. Her performance on the approach still shamed her, but a part of that shame had now hardened into bloodless contempt for their attackers. Dragoon or not —Aeolian or outlander—it made no difference anymore. She was going to make those cannoneers pay.

Vanna spotted the enemy position first. Five heavy cannons on wheeled carts with five rebel fighters manning them—exactly as Senna described. The enemy unit looked as ragged a bunch as she'd ever seen, leather armor beaten and scored, bodies soiled by sweat and discharged gunpowder. She shot across three adjacent treetops to loom over their position, close enough to see the sharp lines their cheekbones carved in their emaciated faces. They all looked like they'd been living in the jungle, foraging to survive.

Not a dagger between them. Out in the open air, her dragoons had been at the mercy of their relentless cannon fire; up close, the ungainly weapons were about as useful as sandbags on a kite-ship.

She signaled back to the wing and the rest of her team fanned out across the canopy.

"Spread and drop," Kendy whispered. "Just like the drill." He gusted over to the treetop next to Vanna, raised his fist, and gave the sign.

Vanna shot out from her perch and drew her rapier mid-air, slicing down at a reckless angle. She gusted to a stop amid all five of the rebel fighters. Ambushed, they panicked. Dragoon fliers brandishing swords and daggers dropped from the treetops, corralling the cannoneers, blocking their paths of escape. Vanna secretly hoped she'd meet with more resistance, but with no small arms to defend themselves, the fighters scattered in wild disarray, all of them yelling in thick Aeolian accents as they crisscrossed the hilltop, attempting to flee.

Kendy and Dray landed last, completing the encirclement. So thwarted, the three panicked fighters who had been the fastest to their feet stumbled over each other as they backed away from the points of sabers and rapiers. Vanna found herself face-to-face with the last of them. It was hard to tell through the soot and soil, but the red-haired fighter looked Zephyri. And young—not a day older than Effie and Kai. Still inflamed, she struck a glancing blow with her rapier across the young fighter's chest. She watched his terrified expression curdle with pain as she drew upon her Gift to blow the legs out from under him.

Gliding forward, she pressed the tip of her rapier against his throat.

"Yield," the boy cried. The mewling sound of him only aggravated her. She pressed the point harder against his throat, clocked the reddening line her blade had drawn across his chest. "Yield!" he screamed again, eyes bugging from his thin face.

"He yields." She heard Kendy's voice behind her, felt pressure on her sword arm from his hand. "Let him up, Lieutenant."

Feeling the battle fever begin to bleed away, Vanna withdrew her rapier and stepped back. Senna and Raji came over to haul the boy up under his arms. They tossed him in a pile with his comrades under guard.

"We need them to talk," Kendy said. "These boys look like Aeolians to me, but they aren't dragoons. That's for sure. We need to understand what's going on here."

Boys. Vanna shielded her face. The other fighters were just as young as the one she'd struck—children playing at soldier, armed with deadly weapons they didn't understand. Her mouth ran sour. She spat, sheathing her rapier.

The dragoons went about dismantling the cannons. When they were finished, Kendy ordered all the barrels rolled off the edge of the island into open sky. She might have been paranoid, but Vanna felt the eyes of all five captives following her around the hilltop.

"They're afraid of you," Kendy said, confirming her suspicions. "Go talk to them. See what you can find out."

Vanna hiked over to the pile of captives, one hand perched by the daggers at her hip. Their bodies drew away from her as she approached, none as terrified as the red-headed boy she'd wounded. He grimaced as he tried to hide behind his comrades. The wound she'd delivered had been a shallow one. He'd make out just fine if it didn't infect, but it had to hurt something fierce.

She grabbed the closest boy by the chin, then tossed him away. "What the hell is this? You know those aren't peashooters you're playing with. Where'd you even get this kind of artillery?"

"B-Bael brought 'em," the boy stammered.

One of his comrades found some fire and elbowed him in the side. "Shut up. She's working for the Shards, idiot."

Vanna drew one of her daggers and smacked the speaker across the bridge of his nose with the flat. "I wasn't talking to you." She turned back to the trembling boy in front of her. "Who's Bael?"

"B-Bael's from ou-outland. C-came to Aeolus to help us deal with the Shards."

"Is that right?" Vanna kept her dagger primed, its tip gleaming with reflected sun. "This Bael tell you to shoot cannons at your fellow Zephyri? He tell you to try knocking dragoons out of the sky?"

"He told us the Shards would send an invasion force—*uhn.*" The boy she had slashed hoisted himself up on one arm with a pained grunt to look at her. "He gave us these cannons—*uhn*—to defend the landing."

"Bael says this is our island!" The boy who had attempted to silence his comrade chimed in. "If we want to keep it, we have to defend it."

Overhearing, Raji stepped up behind Vanna. "Sounds like you boys got some shit advice. These islands belong to our host, and anyone who says otherwise is no better than a pirate."

A pirate. Vanna left the captives and walked over to find Kendy.

"Learn anything?" her commander asked, back from overseeing the final cannon's destruction.

Vanna grunted. "Learned they make little boys as dumb and impressionable out here as anywhere else. They gave up the name of their leader—some outlander called Bael. Sounds like he came here to stir up trouble for our host."

Kendy nodded. "Sire Ansel was right, then. We have to find this Bael and put an end to whatever rebellion he's fomenting."

"Aye," Vanna agreed. "These boys look like they've been hard up in the jungle for some time. We're, what? Twenty leagues from the village?"

Kendy nodded. "Give or take. We were closer at the landing."

"I'll bet the rebels have a camp." Vanna cast her gaze out toward the Aeolian jungle. Though the western island was smaller than Volturnus, its wildlands seemed denser—more vast. "Could be where this Bael's hiding out. Let's go see if they want their boys back."

Kendy agreed to her plan.

Sure enough, the rebels had built an encampment. The boys were only too happy to lead the dragoons to it on the promise of their safe return. "We just want to talk," Vanna said to coax their compliance. "We'll trade you back in exchange for safe parlay. Even pirates respect the rules of parlay."

And so the boys led them at sword point, following the murky course of a jungle creek. The jungle thickened around them. After an hour of marching, they entered a dense gully that cut a serpentine path through the trees. Vanna kept searching the suffocating canopy for any comforting slash of sky but never found it. Dusk came to the jungle nearly as dark as a moonless night. Only then did the winding path through the gully yield to the outlines of a freshwater lagoon.

A rebel scout sighted their party's approach from less than a league out, and Kendy flew ahead to negotiate the terms of the exchange. He rejoined the party looking pale and unsettled.

"What?" Vanna asked. "Don't tell me they won't bargain for the boys —not that I'd blame them." She shot a contemptuous look at their mewling captives, all of whom gathered around Senna accepting mouthfuls of water from her skin.

"No, they'll grant us parlay," Kendy said.

"Then what is it?"

"The scout's a dragoon. He says there are more inside the camp."

Vanna cursed under breath. Kendy's relief had been palpable when they discovered those Giftless little twerps manning the cannons. He allowed himself to believe Sire Ansel's reports might have been in error—that the Aeolus Dragoons *hadn't* turned renegade, *hadn't* set themselves against their host and, through her, the Crystal Throne. This mess was about to get a great deal more complicated than disarming a band of sweaty boys.

Kendy whistled back to Raji and Dray. He'd sent them both up the treetops, tailing the group—insurance against the threat of encirclement. No one knew what they were walking into. There could have been 100 outland rebels camped in the jungle, and there was still the chance these boys were leading them into a trap—however remote.

Vanna's admiration for her commander only grew as this odd mission progressed. His only combat experience up to this point had been the rare intercession runs the Volturnian dragoons made against the lightly armed smugglers who moved between the isles. Here, Commander Kendy Baris faced his first real test of leadership, and he was passing with accolades as far as Vanna saw it. Even Flynn would be proud—if only grudgingly.

"They'll take me and three more up to the camp," Kendy said. "Everyone else will stay and guard the boys to ensure our safe return. Raji. Dray. With me and Vanna. Lya, you have the command here."

Lya returned a confident salute, bowing her blonde head so low Vanna caught a glimpse of twenty some-odd leather bands holding her complicated braids in place.

Dray and Raji sailed over to join the officers' huddle on their Gifts.

"It's a good sign, isn't it?" Dray asked, cracking the calloused knuckles of his sword hand. He alone had the strength of arm to wield a double-edged bastard sword while airborne. The sight of its pommel sticking out over his shoulder brought Vanna some small measure of comfort, however misplaced.

Raji cocked a quizzical eyebrow, prompting Dray to elaborate.

"They only wanted four of us," he clarified. "If they had a pirate army back there all armed to the gills, can't imagine they'd make much hay over eight dragoons versus four."

Another small measure of comfort. However misplaced.

14

VANNA

The rebel camp looked like a sorry place to lay your head—a ramshackle collection of canvas tents hoisted hastily and staked in place with daggers, whittled branches serving as posts. The tents encircled the small lagoon beside the mouth of a natural cave. Warm light twinkled in that cave's arched entrance, flickering behind a curtain of hanging moss like the beaded entrance over the elders' round in Volturnus.

Vanna saw fewer than twenty fighters about the camp, though more might have been deployed elsewhere or cloistered away in their tents. Young boys and girls, mostly—just a smattering of older folk. A few wore the gray flight suit of the Aeolus Dragoons. They looked too much like Vanna's own wing, sporting the same dandelion Crest of Zephyr and next to it, the West Wind of Aeolus—the mirror image of her own home patch. Two of those dragoons looked up from oiling their rapiers as the Volturnians passed. Another stood off to the side, demonstrating how to load a flintlock pistol to a mousey girl who didn't look a day over thirteen.

Not an outlander among them. They all had the straight hair and pale skin of Zephyri. The two or three elders present wore long braids like Flynn. Where were Bael's fighters, then? She found it hard to believe a pirate rabble-rouser landed on Aeolus without his own crew.

She caught pieces of conversation as they passed through the camp.

"...Volturnians, sent by the Shards..."

"...here to speak with Halle."

"Never point it at anyone you don't intend to kill..."

The scout who had become their de facto guide led them to the cave and pointed inside. Kendy nodded back then turned to his team. "You two let me and Vanna do the talking."

"We know why we're here." Dray punched one fist into his open palm. "Just the muscle."

Raji put up his hands, confirming deference.

With one hand on the dagger at his hip, Kendy pushed aside the curtain of hanging moss and led them down a shallow passage, unnaturally lit. The Aeolians had posted liquid braziers along the way, each one flickering with a small flame. The cetacean fat fueling those torches burned smokeless and clean—a canny choice for the unventilated cave, even though they put off a strong fishy odor that churned Vanna's stomach.

An Aeolian accent reached their ears from around a bend in the cave. "You go nose-blind to the ambergris after a while. Beats hiding in the dark."

Something shifted in Kendy's posture when he heard the voice. His hand relaxed over the hilt of his dagger, and he picked up the pace until they came face to face with four rebels seated cross-legged around a vellum map, framed in liquid torchlight.

"Halle!" A hint of relief entered Kendy's voice as he went to greet the familiar Aeolian. Before he got there, the appearance of one of her soldiers stopped him in his tracks.

An Avian fighter stood over the three Aeolian dragoons, so tall its brown-feathered head nearly scraped the ceiling of the cave. The round arches of its folded wings crested over its shoulders, sticking out from a suit of heavy chainmail. Its arms and legs were the most human features of its aspect—even though those legs ended in taloned claws and its hands looked big enough to crush a human head.

"Don't soil your flight suits, now." Halle looked up from her map. "Sparrowhawk has that effect on people, but he's really a gentle bird."

Vanna peeled her eyes away from the Avian and watched Kendy for a cue.

"Does it talk?" he asked.

One yellow eye on the side of Sparrowhawk's head flicked to Kendy. It clicked its beak, filling the cavern with a screeching voice. "*He* talks."

"Come on." Halle waved them over. "I hear you picked up a few of my boys."

With one wary glance at Sparrowhawk, Kendy led his team to sit on the ground opposite their Aeolian counterparts. Vanna took the spot at his right hand, across from a female dragoon with mismatched eyes and tight, pink braids. She recognized the Aeolian from her Ascension and tried to engage the woman with a weak smile, but the gesture wasn't returned. Dray alone kept his feet, sidling off next to Sparrowhawk and puffing out his chest. Vanna assumed he took the Avian's size as a personal affront.

"I'm surprised to see you here, Commander," Kendy said.

Halle rubbed at the thin sheet of pink hair that covered her head like turf. She looked to Vanna like a woman accustomed to a shaved head, only recently forced by circumstance to let her hair reassert itself. "That sentiment cuts both ways," Halle said. "We assumed Kelestina would send in the Armada."

Kendy shook his head. "What's going on here, Commander?"

The younger flier seated across from Vanna interjected, "First, the boys."

"She's right," Halle agreed. "Seeing as we're on opposite sides right now, we need to set the terms of engagement."

"Those boys tried to shoot our wing out of the sky," Vanna cut in. "They nearly killed one of my fliers."

"What?" Halle cursed. "Those idiots. Not half a brain between 'em. I told those shit stains not to fire on fliers. Ships only, I said. Didn't I say that?" Halle unfolded and refolded her legs with a groan. "Why don't you take it from the top, Commander."

Kendy recounted their approach to Aeolus, with Vanna chiming in to provide the details he missed. They didn't mention the kite-ships and the weapons cache they discovered on the skerry.

When they were finished, Halle apologized. "Your man's going to be all right, then?"

"Broken arm," Vanna said. "He'll survive."

"My own fault for setting them up with those cannons. I figured as long as they're shooting at Armada, worst they can do is miss."

Worst they can do? "I don't see how shooting at our host is any better than shooting at dragoons," Vanna said.

"She has a point," Kendy agreed.

Ignoring them both for the moment, Halle pressed on with the negotiations. "So, you'll return them in exchange for parlay?"

"That depends," Vanna said. "You really going to hold us here if we say no?"

Halle's jaw hardened as she looked from Vanna to Kendy. "If I have to. I don't have an army exactly, but I think I've got enough fighters to overpower you lot—especially with Sparrowhawk here."

The Avian gave his wings a threatening ruffle and pointed his beak down at Dray.

"It's fine, Vanna." Kendy put one hand on her shoulder, squeezing. "We don't want your boys, Halle. But you're going to have to find something else for them to do. We gave your cannon barrels the Long Drop."

This seemed to irk Halle, but she extended her hand to shake on it. "Agreed. Safe parlay for the boys."

"What's going on here, Halle?" Kendy asked again.

"And who's Bael?" Vanna added.

Halle raised her hands for them to hold fire. "One question at a time."

The Aeolian Wing Commander launched into a long story that began with the retirement of their former Patrician governor, Dama Anyela. Anyela had been a reasonable magistrate. A bit full of herself in the way of the Celestials' Patrician nobility, but she helped the Aeolians rebuild after Maug's attack and was well regarded around the island. After she left her post and went wherever retired Patrcians go, Kelestina replaced her with a young governor from outland—Sire Muldoon.

Muldoon brought changes to Aeolus. He increased the tithe on grain as well as the port fees. That alone would have been enough to squeeze Aeolus, which had far less agricultural capacity than an island like Volturnus, but Muldoon also commandeered one of the island's two shipyards and set the workers there building craft for the Armada at a steep discount.

"Aeolus isn't like Volturnus," Halle explained. "We rely on commerce to fill our coffers. If we can't build ships or keep our custom at the port, there's nothing left."

"That doesn't sound right." Vanna shook her head. The plebiscite on Volturnus grumbled about the tithe—and the conscripts charged with collection weren't the most popular people in town—but Kelestina's cut was always reasonable. She left everyone with enough to go about their lives unmolested.

Misunderstanding, Halle nodded. "No. It don't. It got to the point where someone had to say something. With the granaries as empty as our coffers, we were looking at a full winter subsisting on forage. That might work in the Spurs, but that ain't enough to feed an island like Aeolus."

"Why didn't you petition Aquilon?" Kendy asked.

"Say, that's a damn good idea," the braided dragoon opposite Vanna chided. "Wish we bred 'em smart on Aeolus like they do on Volturnus. Might have saved this island a lot of trouble if we only knew how to write."

"Shut your mouth, Liv, and that's an order," Halle snapped. "We sent dozens of missives to Aquilon. The elders tried to negotiate with Sire Muldoon. I even went up to his manse a handful of times myself. He just kept saying it was the will of our host, and we were all duty-bound as her guests on these islands to serve it." Two of the liquid braziers burned lower, casting Halle's severe expression in shadow. "That's when Bael arrived. Him and Sparrowhawk came over riding steerage on a merchant ship. Must've slipped in with the barrels. No record of either of them as passengers on the entry log at port."

Vanna had a hard time imagining Sparrowhawk *slipping in* anywhere, but she continued listening to Halle's tale, rapt.

"Bael got in the ear of a few of my dragoons over too many cups of ale. Soon enough, they were all quoting him like some prophet sent by the Jokai. Got sick of hearing it from my corps, so I decided to meet him for myself. I came out to this very camp just like you probably did—planned to give him a piece of my mind and send him off to stir shit elsewhere.

"Thing is—" Halle scratched the pink stubble of her head again, this time searching for the right words. "Bael, right? He's not what you expect. Didn't come here just to stir shit—at least not entirely. Him and Sparrowhawk come from some island called Toran—all the way on the other side of the Doric Sky. They've been dealing with the Celestials a lot longer than we have." She paused again and seemed to meet with some frustration. "*Argh*—I'm no storyteller. It's not going to sound the same coming from me."

Sparrowhawk clicked his beak, turning away from Dray and attending the discussion for the first time. "The Celestials are parasites," he squawked. "They work slowly, like threadworms in your gut. Every kindness they show you is the jeweled scabbard around the dagger of their intent. They'll bleed this land by a thousand cuts. Already, the damage accumulates.

Aeolus is just the first to realize it." His head shifted. One yellow eye landed directly on Vanna. "It will not be the last. Rise up now—while Kelestina idles in her Crystal Palace, isolated from her Armada. Rise up or die."

Vanna stared at Sparrowhawk, aghast. *Treason.* This bird spoke treason. And these dragoons were listening. The situation was even more dire than she imagined. This Bael had turned the plebiscite against their Patrician governor. He'd even poisoned the minds of their dragoons. In this cave, they sat across from the island's *Wing Commander,* and even she appeared to be under this pirate's spell.

Kendy's jaw shifted as Vanna watched him arrive at the same conclusion. "Rise up or die? Halle—this man is a pirate. He's turned you against our host."

Liv sniffed. "What does it say about the Shards that they make us guests on our own islands?"

Halle nodded at that. "I tried giving Sire Muldoon an ultimatum, but he wasn't budging."

"So, you what?" Vanna asked. "Stormed the manse?"

"So to speak," Liv said.

Kendy rubbed his eyes and temples. It had already been a long day, and Vanna sensed they had a ways to go, still. "You have to bring an end to it," Kendy said. "We have our orders from Sire Ansel. If we fail, it *will* be the Armada you're dealing with, and they're not going to want to talk."

"The Celestials need Aeolus," Halle said. "And they need Acolians to make Aeolus work. They're not going to wipe us off the map."

Vanna wasn't so sure. The Celestials didn't need traitors. If the Armada stepped in, Halle's rebels at the very least would be put to the sword. Many others would likely be injured or die in the fighting. This Bael had carved a bloody path for Aeolus.

"I want to speak to Bael," Vanna said. "Why isn't he here?"

Halle smiled with all her teeth, as if this was the request she'd been waiting for. "I think that's a fine idea. Bael's up at the governor's manse, holding our most exposed position. It's too late to fly out there now, but I'll take you to him in the morning. Bring the rest of your wing into camp. We'll set out at dawn."

15

EFFIE

Vanna didn't return the next day, nor the day after that. Effie might have been concerned under different circumstances, but she had her own problems to deal with. The Ascension Ceremony was less than a month away, and she no longer expected her Gift to manifest before Sire Ansel posted the list. That much and more had been laid bare on that humiliating afternoon at the landing with Kai.

The two of them had been avoiding each other ever since, and that meant Effie kept her distance from the bakery. In some ways, she found the isolation liberating. She had a task before her—to qualify for the Ascension—and with so little time to ensure her inclusion, she couldn't afford any distractions. The lists favored the Gifted, but no rule required such a contingency—Effie was certain of it. She just had to find another way to demonstrate her worth and make the case to Sire Ansel for her inclusion on his list.

Careful to avoid the lurking censors—who were already poking around, looking to bind her to some pedestrian task—Effie set out from the village to petition the governor's manse. She escaped the censors unde-tected, but one of Ansel's household conscripts in brass livery stopped her on the flagstone path leading up to his gate. "Can I help you?"

"I'm here to see the governor," Effie said.

The footman looked incredulous. "You... have an audience?"

"I'm requesting one."

"Effie...the governor is a very busy man."

"I think he'll want to hear what I have to say."

The footman sighed. "I'll ask the clerk to make an appointment for you."

Hands clasped, she batted her eyes, all innocence. "Does now work?"

"Now does *not* work." Mild irritation worked wrinkles into the footman's brow. "Sire Ansel is out with his prize mares, and he does not like to be disturbed when he's with his horses."

"Very well, then." Effie curtsied and turned on her heels, pocketing just the information she'd been after.

Sire Ansel might have been a busy man, but he was also a predictable one. He only tended his mares in two places—ensconced in his private stables and along the riding path to Widow's Peak. Trussed up in an unseasonable dress, Effie left the grounds of the manse and scouted a nice flat rock along the scenic trail to sit and wait in ambush.

She waited less than an hour, thumbing a pile of gooseberries in her pocket and rehearsing her lines. The sound of hoofbeats thrumming over beaten ground eventually reached her ears. The governor and his small retinue of conscripted retainers appeared over a distant hill, each seated atop one of his beloved white mares.

Beaming with all the feigned confidence she could muster, Effie hoisted herself off the rock and threw herself in front of the cavalcade.

"Whoa!" Ansel reared his mount. The horse kicked its front legs with a dancer's panache and circled out of its leisurely canter. With his retinue grinding to a halt behind him, Ansel peered around his horse's mane, squinting. "Miss Strait?"

At least he remembers. Effie curtsied, affecting a limp. "Sire—thank the Jokai for their merciful intervention."

Ansel's stony eyes narrowed. "Are you in distress?"

Effie flashed the wincing pout she'd perfected in her bedroom mirror. "I went out this morning to inspect the moonberry crop. The village apothecaries—they like to get a count of the buds to anticipate the upcoming season's yield. For their Nectar. I know I shouldn't have ventured out alone, but it's important work that the apothecaries do—" Sire Ansel's broad-faced expression darkened, and Effie felt his patience wearing thin. *Right to the chase, then.* "I'm afraid I fell while attempting to secure a better vantage from the cliffs. I must have turned an ankle. I hobbled all the way back to the riding path, but the pain has become too great to continue on." She tested another gingerly step and grimaced.

"That was very reckless," Ansel chastised. "You're lucky we found you." He leaned over his horse's ear, and Effie thought she saw him whisper something to the beast. When he looked back up, he nodded to her. "You can ride along on the back of my saddle."

"It won't be too much of a burden?"

Ansel snorted arrogantly. "These are all Ivory Brundisian Mares—bred from the finest stock." He patted his horse affectionately on the side of the neck. "Cloudcutter here could pull a Leviathan. A little slip of a girl will hardly break her back."

"No," Effie giggled. "I don't suppose I will."

Ansel handed his reins to the nearest retainer and leapt from his saddle to help Effie up. Careful to favor her "injured" ankle, she let the governor place his thick hands around her waist and guide her into the stirrup and over the saddle. He mounted in front of her, and she pressed close against his back. Even after a day's riding, the man still smelled of clean leather and smoky perfume.

"Don't be shy," he said. "Cloudcutter's gait is smoother than a eunuch's chin, but it's best to hold on if you're unaccustomed to horseback."

Effie did as she was told as Ansel tugged on his reins to coax Cloudcutter back along the path. She felt his thighs contracting, applying steady pressure, driving the mare into a smooth canter.

Conscious of her limited time before they reached the village, she started in the governor's ear. "Your horses—such remarkable animals. It's like no ride I've ever experienced."

Ansel grunted. "Ridden many horses, have you? On an island without any terrestrial stock?"

"Not many, no," Effie said. "But I've been on the back of a merchant's gelding from Grenport, and I've ample experience with the golden yaks."

"Hardly a comparison." She felt the pressure building in Sire Ansel's legs, the pace of Cloudcutter quickening. He leaned over his mare and Effie could have sworn he whispered something again, though she could not hear him. Cloudcutter returned a snort. "A merchant's gelding hardly rates next to a sporting mare," he said. "And this island's yaks are as dim as a deckhand."

"You sense it, too, then?"

"Hmm?"

"An animal's intelligence. I... *feel* it any time I look upon your mares." Effie affected another girlish giggle. "I'd accept their counsel over half the dullards on Volturnus."

This elicited another snort from Ansel, but this time the sound rang with amusement. "Too true. You sense that, do you?"

Was that a chime of intrigue? Effie hid her own grin behind Ansel's broad shoulders. "I think you know me for a straight talker, Sire. I'm hardly given to hyperbole. The intention in her gait. The way she responds to the slightest pressure. Cloudcutter's much more than a trained beast." She added a slight lilt to her voice to give her rehearsed lines the sound of revelation. "She seems to have more in common with the *dauphine*." Ansel shifted in his saddle at the Leviathan's mention. "And the bond you share," Effie continued. "It seems almost akin to the bond between a Leviathan and a Gifted Pilot."

"Yes..." Ansel peered back at her over his shoulder before returning his attention to the road ahead. "I've had much the same thought."

Effie giggled again, and this time she hardly needed to fake it. She let the ride continue in silence for a time before speaking again—as if the thought had just occurred to her. "I have to admit, I envy your houschold conscripts."

"Hm?"

"To have the privilege of caring for these elegant mares—it's a fine boon you grant them."

"It is," Ansel agreed, then his voice seemed to sour. "Few have the knack for it, truth be told, though I work with what the Jokai grant me."

"Knack is the right word, Sire. A talent inborn that cannot be taught."

"Just so."

"It's just as it is with the Leviathan."

He paused again, but the dangle was well done, and his curiosity got the better of him. "How do you mean?"

"Well, we test our worthiest sons and daughters against the dauphine at the Ascension, but no matter how driven the candidates seem, we so rarely discover any talent."

Ansel spared her another over-the-shoulder glance. "It is a rare Gift." A wiser girl than Effie might have pulled back at the note of suspicion in his voice, but she hadn't the time to dally.

"Rare, yes," Effie agreed. "And even rarer if we aren't looking for it in the right place."

Ansel guided Cloudcutter off the riding path and onto one of the farm roads leading to the village. With her impromptu audience coming to an end, Effie pressed on.

"Of course, it makes sense that we test the strongest Elementalists, but the stories are filled with Leviathan Pilots who possess no additional Gifts—"

"I think that's quite enough chatter, Miss Strait." Ansel clipped her prepared speech. "I'd prefer to finish my ride in silence if you don't mind."

Effie bit down on her lip in frustration. "Of course," she acquiesced pleasantly.

When they finally arrived back at the village gates, Sire Ansel dismounted first and helped Effie out of Cloudcutter's saddle. Careful to favor her allegedly twisted ankle, she limped forward to face him and curtsied.

"I am in your debt, Sire," she said.

"It's nothing. Should I have one of my grooms help you to your cottage?"

"I think I can manage," she said.

"Very well." He turned back to Cloudcutter to remount.

One last card to play. With the governor's back to her, Effie reached into the pockets of her dress and squeezed the overripe gooseberries she'd secreted there. Judging by the regular deliveries of the expensive fruit to Sire Ansel's manse, Effie deduced they must be one of his mares' favored treats. She extended one hand, approaching Cloudcutter, and to her great relief the ivory mare bent to sniff her knuckles then began licking her hand.

Ansel felt the tug on his saddle and looked over, perplexed.

"I think she likes me," Effie said.

Sire Ansel watched her courting the horse and thumbed at his chin, considering. He abandoned his attempt to remount and walked over, cocking his salt-and-pepper head. "Yes... that she does."

"I wonder..." Effie said, one hand flat against Cloudcutter's sweeping tongue, the other softly petting her nose, "...if you might allow me a shift caring for your mares up at the stables? I wouldn't be a bother. I'd love to learn more about their care, and to spend more time with them would be an incredible gift." She patted Cloudcutter one more time and batted her eyes up at Sire Ansel.

Ansel nodded. "I think that could be arranged... You do seem to have a *knack* for it." Effie fought back a smirk as she felt the outlines of her plan boldening. "Once that ankle heals, present yourself at the manse after Fourth Bell. You can assist the lead groom with their afternoon constitutional and feed. Do not be late, mind. Their schedule is very particular."

Effie laughed with honest excitement then threw herself against Sire Ansel, wrapping her arms around his broad body in an ill-advised embrace. He stiffened at the unexpected contact and, for a moment, Effie worried he might push her away. Instead, he awkwardly returned the gesture with a few stiff pats on Effie's back. She felt his calloused hands, rough against her shoulders, bared by the cut of her dress.

"I'm sorry," she said, cautious not to linger. "I'm just so happy. I feel so *drawn* to them."

To her shock, Ansel showed her a fatherly grin. She hadn't thought the Patrician lord capable of such warmth, but she supposed all that formality was another trapping of his authority, nothing more than the emotional livery of his class. Sire Ansel was just a man, after all, like any other. "Do remember not to be late," he said.

She watched him ride away.

16

VANNA

Day broke over the Aeolian jungle. Eight Volturnian dragoons flew in low formation behind Halle's meager delta. They skated over the jungle canopy, charting a course that would bring them into the village before midday.

The sheer expanse of wild land impressed Vanna. By surface area, Aeolus was only half the size of her home island, and yet its jungle must have covered three times as many acres of land.

The humid green canopy eventually gave way to rolling hills and a dun expanse of untamed brush slashed by lines of savannah grass. The dragoons flew for another hour over this landscape before Vanna sighted the first checker-box plots of arable land. A few modest homesteads and rounded granaries poked out from the seams between the fields. Cereal crops mostly, with no florid orchards to supplement. If this was all the agriculture Aeolus yielded, then Vanna had no difficulty believing a heavy tithe might leave the locals wanting.

They set down outside the village before midday. Vanna and Kendy each checked in with their fliers as Halle approached the gates.

"Looked pretty barren," Raji said, lowering his voice.

Vanna had no response, and Halle saved her from finding one by waving the Volturnians to join her.

The gates of Volturnus were almost never barred, but these dragoons had Aeolus sealed up like a village under siege. Two fliers in gray flight suits held the low palisade. Both glided down to lift the bar at their commander's sign, and the heavy wooden gates creaked open.

Halle's report back at the encampment had been dire enough that Vanna had assumed some measure of embellishment. If anything, the Wing Commander had failed to do the situation justice. Few villagers moved freely about the vacant streets, and those Vanna did sight looked just as withered as the boys manning the cannons. Starving features declared themselves on every ashen face they passed, from the distended bellies on four young girls huddled outside a longhouse throwing sticks. The market stalls around the village square lay abandoned but for a butcher selling only jerky and a lone angler hawking saltfish from a fly-infested vat. Even the port looked vacant, its landings abandoned, what few vessels remained, forgotten on their moorings.

"We closed the port," Halle said. "Bael warned us the Shards might attempt passing infiltrators off as merchants."

Bael again. Perhaps infiltration *was* a risk, but closing the port only exacerbated the local famine, a condition that would have driven the Aeolians deeper into this pirate's embrace.

On the other hand, Vanna could not deny the privation she'd now witnessed with her own two eyes. This much suffering accumulated over time. She couldn't attribute it all to the embargoed port.

The governor's manse loomed over the village from a low hilltop on the inland edge of the palisade. It looked just like the plot Sire Ansel had selected for his own redoubt, but the structure's design was more severe—like the hilt of a great weapon buried in the Aeolian stone. Where Ansel's manse looked more like a glorified hunting lodge, Muldoon's had been built from sterner stuff—flagstones and firebrick and some unusual roofing of overlapping tiles. Vanna saw no thatch here, no timbers cut from the island's trees. Two spires flanked the entryway, each one rising a third story above the rest of the manse.

Halle pushed open the heavy front door and moved unimpeded through the building, following a path described by a long white runner embroidered with rectangular patterns of ebony and gold. She led the procession through the empty foyer and into a receiving room featuring lofted ceilings and a masoned throne. The high seat's aspect unsettled Vanna even more than the esoteric design.

Navigation maps hung like art from the walls—a few that Vanna recognized and many more that looked copied out of myth.

Halle stepped up to an arched doorway behind the throne over which hung one of the more unusual sky charts annotated in a language Vanna couldn't decipher. "I don't want to overwhelm him." Halle placed her hand on the iron door handle. "Only you two beyond this point." She pointed at Kendy and Vanna. "The rest of y'all can wait here. And don't sit on that stupid throne—it's bad luck."

The outnumbered Aeolian dragoons closed ranks, sizing up their Volturnian counterparts. Vanna spared them a guarded look before following Kendy up to the door.

Halle knocked three times before letting herself inside. Over the Aeolian commander's shoulder, Vanna caught her first glimpse of a small study filled with sturdy tables and ringed by shelves of books. Heat wafted out from the room, expressed by a small fire flickering in a windowed hearth. The wood-burning stove stood on clawed feet in the corner of the room. Vanna scanned the walls as she followed Halle inside, eyes touching the outlines of a dozen more framed sky charts—several depicting the familiar shores of the Zephyr Isles. The centerpiece was a calligraphic atlas painted over three panels joined by a hinged wooden frame. The triptych's center panel described the outlines of the Doric Sky—that vast expanse of open blue in which the Zephyr Archipelago was but a collection of dust. Hundreds of islands populated the triptych's leaflets, some of a size and character with the Zephyrs and others far vaster and more remote. A few had been outlined by the cartographer in red dye and annotated with signs Vanna recognized as wind vectors.

She lingered on the atlas, nearly forgetting the two men who sat at the craftsman table beneath its gilt frame.

"Kelestina took a swing, just like you said she would," Halle announced, stepping aside to present Kendy and Vanna. "Here's the swing."

Both men looked up from a ledger book they'd been studying. The first, a balding Aeolian wearing the governor's brass livery looked much like the plebeians conscripted into Ansel's service. The other, however—he would have stood out on any street in the archipelago.

Bael looked to be about Kendy's age, approaching thirty. His smooth chestnut skin recalled a Patrician lord more than the poxy sailors who shipped into the Volturnian port all blistered and burned from long months baking under the harsh sun of the open sky. His pale blue hair and thin mustache matched the tint on the triptych atlas hanging above. It was a coloring unknown to the Zephyri, and if that hadn't been enough of a foreign tell, his hair was coarser than any Vanna had ever seen. He kept it braided in a plot of cornrows, the ends of each braid knotted at the back of his thick neck with a black leather band.

He stood up from the table, revealing a lean frame and six-foot stature that made him seem oversized for the low-ceilinged room. "They seem harmless enough," Bael observed, smiling affably as he stepped forward and extended his hand, first to Vanna. "Bael of Kensha," he said. "The Bluethorn to my comrades and Serpenttongue Bael to—well—" he scratched the back of his braided head and looked down, "—to those less inclined to comradery."

"Vanna Strait," she answered. "Draft Lieutenant of the Volturnus Dragoons." She met his hand to sanctify the exchange, and to her great surprise he lifted it to his mouth and kissed her gently across the knuckles. Vanna froze, her hand pressed against this outlander's pursed lips as he probed her with hazel eyes.

"And I am the Wing Commander of the Volturnus Dragoons—Kendy Baris." Kendy forced himself between them and forcefully shook Bael's hand.

Bael accepted Kendy's hand, though his almond eyes lingered on Vanna. During the exchange, Halle had worked her way around the room and was now looking down at the ledger abandoned on the table. "Not that anyone cares at this point, but this is Tyson." She gestured at the balding Aeolian in livery. "Tyson used to keep the books at the port. Sire Muldoon conscripted him to work as the village treasurer."

Kendy acknowledged Tyson with a nod, but Vanna remained transfixed by Bael. Here was the man who had talked his way inside the ranks of the Aeolian Dragoons—who had used his influence to foment rebellion. *Serpenttongue, indeed.* She'd been expecting a visage more like Maug's— black-bearded and crisscrossed with scars.

"You dragoons," Bael said, seeming to address only her. "Remarkable creatures. Gifts I have not seen on either side of the Doric Sky. And *so many* Gifted—it is a rare thing. I can certainly see why the Celestials took an interest."

His genuine admiration left Vanna disarmed. She wished she could channel some of Effie's stubbornness—use it as an anchor to keep herself from drifting off course. "It's not the Celestials' interests that brought us across the sky to Aeolus," she ventured.

Bael's face ignited with amusement. "An incisive mind to match her beauty and Gifts. Draft Lieutenant—you already had me piqued, but now you have my attention."

Vanna groaned, hoping the heat rising in her cheeks would not betray her. She peered around Bael at Kendy, who had joined Halle and Tyson over the books. Bael noticed her interests shifting and stood to the side, extending one arm with the other folded behind his back. "Shall we join them?"

"Here you can see where it changed." Halle pointed to a page in the ledger, interrupting Tyson's rambling explanation.

"Midsummer, the Thirteenth Year of our Host," the treasurer prattled on. "Yields dipped within expected fluctuations, but you'll see here the governor's tithe actually *increases* in real terms as well as a percentage of yield. The excise on port fees nearly *doubled* over the same period of time."

Kendy flipped through the pages of the ledger, glancing over each column.

"The story's all there—plain to see." Bael stood back from the table as if he'd already memorized the ledger from rote. "A new phase of the Celestials' occupation begins. Kelestina has fattened you up like hogs, protected you from the wolves in the hills. Now begins the time for slaughter."

Kendy looked up at Vanna, shaking his head—*it doesn't look good*.

"Let's say Kelestina *has* been throttling Aeolus." Vanna unconsciously moved her hand over her daggers, acutely aware that Halle stood just an arm's length behind her. "What do *you* have to gain from interfering? What even brought you to Aeolus—to the archipelago? You're not from anywhere around here and neither is your Avian friend."

"Ah! You've met Sparrowhawk—"

"This isn't a joke to us," Vanna said. "Kelestina sent us to put down this rebellion you incited, and that's still what we're planning to do. *Her* motivations, I understand. It's yours I just can't fathom."

Kendy stood up from his hunch over the table and sidled next to Vanna with nothing to add but his own presence to buttress her question. Bael looked at both the Volturnian dragoons and nodded, thoughtfully pawing at one end of his thin blue mustache. After a moment's consideration, he turned to the triptych atlas hanging over the table.

He pressed one finger down on a small spec of land on the eastern shore of the Doric Sky. Vanna couldn't read the calligraphic script on the atlas, but she knew that he pointed to Aeolus. "We're here," Bael said. He slid his finger an inch to the northeast. "Kelestina is here. On Aquilon." He tapped the northerly Zephyr Island, then suddenly dragged his finger across the wide expanse of the Doric Sky. He stopped over a small Celestial character marking a peninsula jutting off from an island so large it extended beyond the triptych's central panel and onto the western leaflet. "I'm from here. Kensha. A mid-sized city-state in the Toran Federation. He touched three more spots on the map, each one labeled with the same calligraphic character. "Each of these is a Crystal Palace just like Kelestina's. The Celestials call them *consulates*, though I wouldn't be surprised if none of you have heard that name. The occupation in this land is still young. We are not so lucky.

"The first Armada expedition ship made landfall in Toran nearly sixty years ago. My people have been waging a war of attrition against the Celestials ever since." The cast of his eyes became graver as he locked gazes with Kendy and Vanna—lingering again, it felt, on her. "We're not winning. The Celestials have outposts across the Doric Sky and elsewhere. Some of the strategos in Toran suspect their reach extends across all Eight Skies of Ciel."

"You're our enemy, then." Kendy's brow had drawn tighter and tighter over the course of Bael's geography lesson until, finally, the tension forced him to interject. "We are subjects of the Crystal Throne. Give us one reason why we shouldn't haul you and Sparrowhawk back to Aquilon and toss you at Kelestina's feet to meet her judgment?"

Bael set his hands on his narrow hips. The man was built like a rapier. "Because I don't think we are enemies at all—no, no. I think we are allies fighting the same war. You Volturnians just haven't realized it yet."

"The increased tithe—" Halle cut in. "We had Tyson check the ledgers against the records at the port. None of the food is going up to Aquilon like you'd expect. It's all shipping across the deep sky alongside those kite-ships Sire Muldoon's building at the commandeered shipyard."

Bael nodded along, adding, "The Celestials are using colonies like the Zephyr Isles to support the war effort against *my* people—in Toran. The armies of the Federation are doing all they can to fight back at home, but my organization has a different agenda."

"Your organization?" Vanna felt her eyebrows drifting toward her bangs.

"We call ourselves the Gulliver Ring," Bael offered. "Our people cannot win a conventional war against the Crystal Throne, so my associates believe we need a different strategy. Operatives like me—we infiltrate the Celestials' outlying colonies before they can get a foothold. Our goal is to empower the local populations—to liberate the plebiscite. In so doing, we dam the streams feeding the Armada in Toran. Starve the Armada and save the people in the process." His smile returned, too easy for the moment. "It's a reasonably noble goal, if I do say so myself."

"The Celestials came for us first," Halle added. "Doesn't mean they won't be coming for you. To hear Bael tell it, the Shards got good at running this racket. Volturnus is the only power in the archipelago that could threaten Aquilon. Kelestina knows this. She's going to keep you lot happy as long as she can and pick the rest of us off around you."

The bitterness in Halle's voice chilled Vanna. The Aeolian wing commander had already started to see Bael as the ally here and her fellow dragoons as the threat. It was going to be difficult to reset that alignment by argument alone. Aeolus was undeniably suffering, and Bael offered relief. She and Kendy had to offer the equivalent or better if they were going to break this man's hold on the island without a fight.

"Let's say we believe any of this," Kendy allowed. "What could an empire as vast as the one you're describing need from the Zephyr Isles? We barely produce enough food to sustain our own populations—as that ledger proves. Grenport's shipyards are ten times the size of Aeolus'. The quarry on Avernus is less than a gravel pit. Just ask the outland mining crews who transport its yield."

"Everything you say is true," Bael agreed, once again stroking the end of his mustache. "But you have one thing on these remarkable islands the Celestials covet above all else—yes?" Again, his eyes touched Vanna.

You dragoons—remarkable creatures.

"Elementalists," Vanna realized out loud. "We have Gifts."

Bael's smile reached the corners of his almond eyes. "The Celestials fancy themselves collectors of the Gifted. Just look at their Patrician class— each one of them an elevated plebeian with an unusual Gift. The Elementalist powers endemic to these islands would be appealing enough for Kelestina to set up a consulate—but the potential to discover Gifted *Pilots* for their Leviathan fleet? That's worth more than all the gold in Rogerbar-ron's Horde."

The Ascension Ceremony. It was the one occasion that brought Kelestina down from her seat at Aquilon to mix with her plebeian guests. She'd introduced the rite the same year her Armada drove Maug from their shores—her only cultural injection aside from their rigid caste system. Bael's story fit too neatly with their own—like a hidden leaflet unfolded against the unfinished triptych of their lives. As uneasy as he made her, she could not deny him outright.

"Halle," Kendy said. "Can we speak privately?"

The Aeolian commander folded her arms and sat back in her seat across from Tyson. "Anything you have to say, you can say in front of Bael."

Vanna felt Kendy's posture stiffen beside her as he likely came to the same realization she had just moments before. *They* were the outsiders here. Not Bael.

"We can't deny what you say has the ring of truth," Vanna interjected. "And I can certainly understand why you'd want to save your land from war. Our islands have seen violence... but it was the Celestials who delivered us from those torments. We *cannot* throw that blood debt away on an outlander's insinuations." She turned to Halle then. "If we can reduce the tithe to its previous rate and restore your shipyard, would you bring an end to this occupation?"

Halle's lips folded into a frown as she considered. To her credit, she didn't glance over at Bael for any kind of permission. "I'd have to consider it...talk it over with the elders and the other dragoons."

"We'll need to speak with Sire Muldoon," Vanna continued. The gover-nor's mention stirred something in both Halle and Bael.

Kendy noticed it, too. *"Jokai fend*—you didn't kill the man, did you?"

"Sky's blessing, no!" The treasurer, Tyson, looked aghast at the very suggestion.

"I could take you to him. If you would accept my escort?" Bael's smile had returned after its momentary lapse.

Vanna pulled Kendy off to the side and spoke to him in a dragoon's Gifted whisper, conducting air currents to carry barely audible words from one's lips to the other's ear.

"I'll talk to the governor and hear the other side of this," Vanna said.

"You stay with Tyson and Halle and figure out a plan to unwind all the damage that's been done."

"Agreed," Kendy whispered back. "But take Dray to watch your back. I don't trust this man."

Her eyes touched upon the outlander again, who was watching her in return.

"Nor I," she whispered back.

17

VANNA

Bael led Vanna to the village gaol where they kept Sire Muldoon under rotating dragoon guard. As soon as the doors swung open, the stench struck like a cannon's leaden report. She spotted the prisoner huddled in one corner of his cell, unmoving. Muldoon still wore his fine Patrician suit, though its brassy trim had become tarnished by layers of filth and squalor. The nobleman's sweep of brown hair hung limp over his emaciated face, which he shielded, huddling against the cold stone wall with neither pillow nor pallet to support him.

"You boys can leave us, please." Bael signaled to the two cadet dragoons guarding the governor's cell. They complied as if the order came directly from their commander.

Vanna pulled the high collar of her flight suit over her face and pushed past Bael, edging as close to the cell as she could without gagging. The governor did not stir at the sound of Bael's arrival, nor did he lift his sunken face to meet Vanna's. All the reek came from the piled waste and pools of urine darkening the opposite corner of the cell. Beside the midden, a soiled white cravat repurposed as a wipe lay discarded.

"You're torturing him," Vanna said.

The outlander sniffed, unmoved by the accusation. "Hardly. We're simply keeping him in the same conditions he'd have the Aeolians suffer."

"I doubt he denied the entire island their privies," Vanna shot back.

Bael conceded the point with a shrug. "We feed him twice a day... but not before taking our *tithe*." He smiled acidly, the ends of his blue mustache rising over his cheekbones. Vanna saw something unsettling in that expression. A man so convinced of his own justice was a dangerous thing. "He's just lucky we caught him over land," Bael continued. "Sky Law says collaborators get the Long Drop."

A ragged choking sound rose up from the heap of Sire Muldoon. The governor's hunched back shook with every repetition. Vanna watched him hucking and gasping, slow to identify the sound as laughter.

"A pirate, after all." Muldoon's voice sounded hoarse, though it still rang with that gilded Patrician accent. "You reveal yourself, Bael of Kensha."

The governor looked up. The ineffable set of youth on his drawn face shocked Vanna to attention. Muldoon's wide-set almond eyes still held the sparkle of vitality, even churning as they were amid a sea of pallor. His narrow face ended in a prominent chin, and despite the obvious pains of captivity, not a wrinkle creased his brow. She knew little and less about what it took to become a Patrician lord of the Crystal Throne. Sire Ansel had seen over fifty summers, but Muldoon appeared half that age. Vanna pulled closer to the cell, sensing something of a challenge in this young Patrician's emergent gaze.

"You've got a visitor," Bael said, addressing Muldoon. "Now be nice and answer her questions. This dragoon didn't fly all the way from Volturnus just to sniffle your filth."

"Volturnus?" Muldoon's lips curled. "Welcome to Aeolus." He cocked his head, reading the bronze-wing patch on her flight suit. "Lieutenant, is it? Come to rescue me from these villains?"

"Something like that." Vanna's eyes drifted to the excrement piled in the corner of the cell. "I'm sorry for the way you've been treated."

Rage finally cracked Muldoon's tired expression. "It is... *unfortunate*," he said, quickly reasserting his composure.

Vanna turned back to Bael. "I'll speak to the governor alone."

The outlander shook his braided head. "I'm afraid I can't allow it."

"You're in no position to argue. We still haven't decided what to do with you."

"Is that right?" Bael crossed his arms.

Vanna stood firm. "The only sword you've got is huddled in the jungle miles away from here. I've got ten fully armed dragoons in the village. I like our chances."

"Ahoy! Fire to match her beauty, wit and Gifts." Bael laughed heartily, tweaking the ends of his blue mustache. If anything, the threat seemed to titillate him. "I tell you what, Lieutenant. I'll give you ten minutes—one for each of those *fully armed dragoons*."

And with that, Bael exited the gaol, leaving Vanna and the prisoner alone.

Hearing the gaol door slam in the wake of Bael's reluctant exit, Muldoon straightened his back, but did not approach—mere distance the only cover afforded him. For a Volturnian who spent the majority of her life inside the rigid hierarchy of the Celestials' social strata, it felt indecent to look upon a Patrician lord so abased. The inversion nauseated Vanna as much as the stench. Vanna served at the pleasure of their host and her appointed governor. Patrician lords were immune to local tribunal— empowered to levy taxes, apportion labor, conscript staff... A governor's word was as good as law on the Zephyr Isles, backed with deference by the plenary seat on Aquilon. Bael had twisted this social order on Aeolus. In this cell, Muldoon was but a man, and his very fate now turned on the judgment of a low plebeian—a mere dragoon. In this room, all those rigid lines of power that cut across Vanna's life bent and intersected.

"It took you long enough," Muldoon sneered. "I've been locked in here for over a fortnight. Why isn't that pirate in chains?"

"I have a few questions, Sire."

That only seemed to irritate the governor. He cast his eyes up to the low stone ceiling of his cell and sighed. "Will the indignities never end?"

Vanna pressed on. "We had a look at your ledgers up at the manse. The changes you've made have brought substantial suffering to Aeolus."

"As is my right," Muldoon snapped, sounding almost peevish. "Tell me, Lieutenant, by what right do you dare invade my private offices? Who granted you the authority to audit my ledgers?"

"The authority—"

"*Authority*, Lieutenant," he cut her off. "I trust you understand the word? *My* authority derives directly from our host, Her Lightness Kelestina of Aquilon."

Vanna choked back a sharp retort. This was not how she expected their conversation to go. She supposed she couldn't blame the governor if his present predicament left him short on patience. "I think you misunderstand something, Sire."

"I misunderstand?" He sprayed her with another round of jagged laughter. "I'm the one shitting on the floor in a plebeian gaol cell. What could I possibly have misunderstood about the situation?"

Each time the governor opened his mouth, Vanna felt her sympathy bleeding away. Patrician or not, this man needed a reminder that his fate turned on her judgment. "We didn't come here to rescue you, Sire. Governor Ansel sent the Volturnian Dragoons to Aeolus to end the rebellion."

"I see no distinction—"

"Well, I do." Vanna liked the way his pale face reddened when she paid back the interruption. "It seems to me that your mismanagement of the island is at the very root of this unfortunate situation. As we speak, my wing commander is going over your ledger with his Aeolian counterpart. They're going to devise a system that will unwind your egregious tithe, restore control of the port and the shipyard you've commandeered so the plebiscite can continue to thrive. If you want to bring an end to this rebellion, you need to sign off on their reparations."

The way he looked at her then—like a dragoon staring down a horsefly, aghast such a measly thing had the gall to bite him. If Muldoon had hoped to find in Vanna some unrepentant salvation, then that misapprehension was quickly vanishing. The moment of cruel revelation hung pregnant between them.

"No," he finally said after a long pause. He shrank back to the corner opposite his midden.

"No?"

"No," he repeated, without further elaboration.

"Sire—your taxes are bleeding Aeolus to death. Surely, this can't be the best way to serve our host."

With an animal growl that was distinctly un-Patrician, Muldoon lunged back up and threw himself against the bars of his cell. "This rabble are all *guests* of the Crystal Throne—except for that vile Kenshan pirate and his half-breed. *I decide* how Aeolus can best be of use to our host." Seething, Sire Muldoon bared his ivory teeth, the only part of him untarnished by his captivity. "Your plebeian mind can't possibly conceive of the Throne's designs. The interests of our host span the breadth of the Doric

Sky, and it is a Patrician magistrate's duty to wring value from our subject guests. Every. Last. Drop. That is how a Patrician distinguishes himself to the Celestial Court."

Vanna backed away. Muldoon's temperament was unlike anything she'd witnessed from Sire Ansel or any Patrician of Kelestina's court. Such *venom*—it leaked from his every entitled outburst. With little goading, he revealed himself to be exactly the threat that Bael described. And where did that leave her, the one stuck standing between them?

"You can't leave me here," Muldoon stated plainly. "You can't return to Volturnus and tell your governor you sided with the pirates who captured and *profaned* a fellow Patrician lord. Release me." He wrapped his hands around the bars of his cage. "*Release me this instant.*"

"Knock knock." Bael interrupted at just the opportune moment. "Time's up."

With one last look at Sire Muldoon's sneering face pressed between the bars of his cell, Vanna turned to leave the gaol.

"You have no choice," he called after her.

"What happened?" Bael asked as she passed him.

She only shook her head. "I need to speak with my commander."

She found him at the tavern where the rest of her wing had assembled, reunited with Hal and Prestor. They'd spent the day reconnoitering the village and came to much the same conclusion Kendy discovered in Sire Muldoon's books. The public house remained busy with commerce. Even if the granaries had suffered, there seemed to be no shortage of ale.

"Never seen such a sorry lot," Hal said. "It's as bad as it was after the Butcher came through—worse in some ways."

"It's all there in the ledgers," Kendy confirmed. "This governor—he's strangling Aeolus to death. We can unwind it, but it's going to take time to repair the damage. What did you get from Sire Muldoon? Is he well?"

"He's alive," Vanna said.

Kendy nodded. "At least that's something. Will he accept a resolution?"

"I didn't get that impression..." Vanna felt the eyes of her wing on her —including Kendy's. They looked to her for an obvious solution. She found herself wishing for Effie's counsel in that moment. Her sister had a way of thinking around conflicts that seemed otherwise intractable. It was as good as a Gift in Vanna's eyes, even if Effie never saw it that way.

What would Effie do?

"We can't leave Bael in charge of Aeolus," she ventured. Kendy nodded along, but some of the other fliers didn't look so convinced. "We can't let Sire Muldoon reinstate the tithe, either. Commander Halle won't have it. Even if we force the issue, how long can Aeolus survive with its governor at war with the island's dragoons?"

"What do you suggest, then?" Kendy cocked an eyebrow across his tankard of ale.

"My sister," Vanna prefaced. "She says the best resolution is often the one that leaves everyone in a fit."

"Sounds...counterintuitive," Raji mused.

"Sounds like Effie," Kendy added.

Vanna began circling the outlines of a plan, speaking it as it occurred to her. "Let's leave everyone in a fit—Halle, Bael, Ansel, Muldoon—all of 'em. Only Aeolus comes out ahead."

"What are you suggesting?"

"Revert the ledgers as planned," she said. "Leave it up to Halle to implement. Without the tithe, this island has no reason to keep harboring Bael and his serpent tongue. The dragoons need to banish Bael. In exchange, we'll take Muldoon back to Volturnus to receive Sire Ansel's judgment. We don't have the authority to punish a Patrician lord, so let Kelestina decide what to do with him."

Kendy took a long draft from his tankard.

"It does make some sense..." Hal said, adjusting his sling to prop his splinted arm up on the table. "I'm in no condition to fly. I can stay behind and make sure Halle follows through."

Vanna tilted her own tankard in thanks, then looked back to Kendy. "It's your decision, Commander. But I don't see any other way through that doesn't end in a sword fight."

Drumming his fingers on the tavern table, Kendy checked the gathering of Aeolian dragoons off in another corner of the tavern. Halle sat among them, drinkless and watching the Volturnian summit, intensity hooding her eyes.

"Can't say I have a better idea," Kendy submitted. "Let's see if Halle hates it just enough to accept."

18

EFFIE

Effie appeared at Sire Ansel's manse the next day, just after Fourth Bell, as instructed. Her time was running short.

She explained away her ankle as a mere bruise, nearly healed by a night of elevation and ice from the butcher's bin. The footman listened to her tale, disinterested, then directed her to the lead groom who put her to work mucking stalls and preparing the mares' feed.

The mixture required a careful balance of millet, gooseberry pulp, and —to Effie's surprise—an amber spirit that smelled like the apothecary's shop.

"You must be cautious to fully macerate the berries and drain the juice," the lead groom chided. "If the pith is too chunky or the mixture too wet, the mares will reject the entire batch, and you'll have to begin again from scratch."

It was as bad as scut work in Effie's mind, but she applied herself to the tasks with feigned good humor, cautious not to elicit any ill report that might reach Sire Ansel's ears.

On her third day at the stables, she caught her first sighting of the governor. It was nearing the end of her shift after all the mares in the stable had been watered and fed. Effie lingered next to Cloudcutter's stall, determined to force a relationship with the stubborn beast.

"Miss Strait." Ansel acknowledged her with a courtly bow. "I trust you're finding the work rewarding."

"Oh yes, Sire. I'm trying hard not to pick favorites, but I keep finding my way back to Cloudcutter's side."

Ansel came over and picked up a handful of the feed that Effie had just meticulously mixed. He fed Cloudcutter from his palm and patted her neck. "She's a special one, I do agree."

"Sire..." Effie ventured. "I thought I might have a word."

He looked down at her, still doting on his mare. "Yes?"

"It's about something we discussed on our ride—after you rescued me from the twisted ankle."

"Healing well, I see."

"Yes." Effie recognized the danger in this next play. She'd be wise to wait a little longer, but time was not a luxury she could indulge in. "It's about the Ascension Ceremony. The Leviathan."

Ansel stopped petting Cloudcutter and turned to study Effie, his expression revealing nothing of his mind.

"As you might know, I turned sixteen this past year and to my unending shame I've yet to manifest an Elementalist Gift." Ansel's nostrils flared as he exhaled, but he didn't stop her. "I know that you look to the Gifted first and foremost when constructing your list for the ceremony, but I can't help but wonder if that leaves some of us Giftless plebeians...overlooked? I've accepted that I might not be an Elementalist, but the dauphine call to me... It's just like it is with your mares."

"Miss Strait, it's hardly appropriate—"

She dared to cut him off. "I know it is important to our host to identify potential Pilots. If I'm not permitted the opportunity to—to *test* myself against the dauphine—I believe with all my heart it will be a dire waste of potential."

Ansel's eyes narrowed, and Effie saw the gears turning. Did he suspect this had all been a ruse, a carefully manicured trail leading up to this point?

Cloudcutter snorted and Ansel turned to tend her. "You have some nerve, I'll give you that," he said. "I can't remember any Giftless plebeian outright petitioning for the right to Ascend."

"That's what I'm telling you, Sire," Effie said. "I'm not like any other plebeian."

A winded footman suddenly burst into the stable, interrupting their conversation at its most tender point. The portly servant had sweat through his livery. He looked like he'd run the distance from the manse out to the stables.

"Sire—" the footman wheezed. "I'm sorry to interrupt. I know—*huff*—that you don't like to be interrupted—*huff*—from your mares—"

"Out with it, man," Ansel said, and Effie couldn't tell if his impatience was with her or this servant's staggered report.

The footman took a deep breath and exhaled the rest of his message. "The dragoons have returned from Aeolus."

"Very well," Ansel replied, waving one dismissive hand. "Have them brought to the manse for debrief."

"They're already here," the footman said. "The Draft Lieutenant landed a kite-ship on the lawn."

"She *what?*" Ansel's eyes bugged from his heavy brow as he rounded back on the footman.

The footman flinched away, bobbing his head. "I think you'll want to receive them with some urgency, Sire."

Without a word for Effie or Cloudcutter, Sire Ansel stormed out of the stables in pursuit of this footman's report. Quickly removing her gloves and smock, Effie tore after him to see just what the commotion was all about.

Vanna had returned. *Of course, it was Vanna.* Who else would come crashing through the culminating moment of Effie's delicate plan?

She found her sister right where the footman described, standing next to a kite-ship that she certainly hadn't taken on her way off Volturnus. Vanna looked like a valkyrie out of legend in her ruffled flight suit, brow sparkling with sweat, violet hair tossed by the turbulence of flight. She stood over a bound man, clearly her prisoner. He knelt, disheveled at Vanna's feet, hands tied behind his back with rope that looked like it had been cut from the kite-ship's moorings. A limp mop of auburn hair concealed the captive's eyes as he knelt on the lawn between Vanna and Ansel. His attire might have been a Patrician uniform once, but it was difficult to tell beneath all the accumulated layers of tatter and filth.

Ansel faced Vanna and her captive across the expanse of his landscaped foreyard, and Effie ducked behind a topiary bush to watch the confrontation play out.

"Lieutenant Strait—" Ansel's voice sounded tight, a lyre string on the verge of snapping. "What is the meaning of this? Where is Commander Baris?"

"The rest of the wing should be back at the village by now, recovering from the flight." Vanna blew a stray lock of hair from her face. "I didn't want to waste any time bringing you news of our resolution. And this..." She grabbed her captive by the hair and held his head up for Ansel to inspect.

"*Muldoon?*" Ansel sputtered.

The captive's contemptuous expression chilled Effie to the bone.

Vanna released the man and nodded. "I figured you'd met, Sire. The rebellion on Aeolus is quelled. I bring you the man responsible."

Effie watched Ansel look back and forth between Vanna and Muldoon, grasping for any hint that might explain this spectacle. "My report said there were pirates—" he started

Vanna nodded again. "They've been dealt with, as well, but the fault rests with the Lord Governor. His greed brought Aeolus to the brink."

Effie gasped and quickly slapped a hand over her mouth. *The Lord Governor? Jokai fend, Vanna had arrested a Patrician of Kelestina's court!*

Ansel's shifting stare came to rest on the abased Muldoon. "This is not what we discussed," he muttered, voice sinking to a growl.

"Sire—you asked us to bring a quiet end to the rebellion. Aeolus had no peaceful path forward with this man in control. The ports are open again. The shipyards are back at work. The pirates have been chased from her shores."

"You must release this man, Lieutenant," Ansel said, still studying Muldoon with that offended cast to his gaze.

"Gladly." Vanna reached for the dagger at her belt and quickly cut the ropes binding Muldoon's hands. The prisoner fell forward onto his hands, expression hidden behind a curtain of limp hair. "I turn the false Governor Muldoon over to you and our host for judgment. You all can figure out what to do with him." With that, Vanna affected a curt bow to Sire Ansel. "The rebellion on Aeolus is quelled."

19

EFFIE

Effie snuck away from the grounds surrounding Sire Ansel's manse and followed Vanna back to the village. With all the commotion of the dragoons' return from Aeolus, she doubted she'd be missed.

She almost couldn't believe what she'd witnessed. It was unheard of. The Patrician caste didn't answer to the plebiscite; not even the dragoons possessed the authority to make such an arrest. Beyond the appalling breach of etiquette, Vanna had interrupted Effie's careful ploy at its most sensitive moment. She doubted she'd have another ripe opportunity to get in Sire Ansel's ear before he made his list for the Ascension. She'd have to hope she made enough of an impression already. Her case had always been weak, but she'd laid it out as best she could—done everything in her power to demonstrate what made her such a worthy gamble.

Vanna hadn't returned home by the time Effie reached the village. On a hunch, she hiked out to the landing and found her sister standing next to Kendy amid a gathering of uniformed dragoons. Effie counted all the fliers who set out for Aeolus minus two—Prestor and Hal. Her throat felt suddenly dry.

"Where are the others?" Effie demanded, thrusting herself into the center of the gathering. "Prestor? Hal?"

The haggard wing of dragoons parted so that Effie could face her sister.

"Effie, what are you—"

"Tell me what happened to Prestor and Hal!" she demanded.

"They're fine," Kendy said. "Hal's got a busted wing, but they're both safe on Aeolus."

Effie breathed, finding her way back to composure. She pointed one accusatory finger at the bronze-wing patch on Vanna's chest. "I saw that scene you made in Sire Ansel's foreyard!"

Vanna shook her head, confused. "How—"

"It doesn't matter," Effie snapped. "Have you lost your damned mind?"

"Whoa, there." Kendy moved to break them up, but both sisters waved him off, closing with each other.

"You assaulted a Patrician lord, Vanna! Do you have any idea what this means?"

"Do *you*?" Vanna's question dripped with so much exhaustion and condescension that it drove Effie back, flat on her feet. "Don't lecture me, Eff. You weren't on the mission. You aren't even a dragoon. You don't have the first clue about the complications—the interests we needed to balance!"

"Is that what you were doing? Balancing interests?" Effie looked from Vanna to Kendy and back again. The other dragoons stood stone-faced, bearing silent witness to the sudden tirade. "You made the wrong decision, Vanna. We are *guests* on these islands. Do you not understand that? Sire Ansel sent you out to Aeolus to restore order. Instead, you've gone and kicked over the entire berry cart." She brought her hands together in mock applause. "Honestly, Vanna—is there anything besides wind between those ears?"

Vanna's tired expression darkened, a fell composure displacing her exhaustion and rage. She stepped toward her sister until they stood nearly nose to nose. Vanna had mere inches on Effie, but in that moment she stood as tall as any dragoon on Volturnus. "Everyone's had enough of this self-important game you're playing, Eff—me, most of all."

"Excuse me?"

Vanna wasn't finished. "Who do you think you're fooling? Sucking up to Sire Ansel doesn't make up for the fact that you're Giftless. It makes you a whore."

The insult struck Effie as painfully as if Vanna had buried that dagger in her flesh to the hilt. She stepped back, eyes burning as she waited for the tears to well, but none came.

That's right, she remembered. *I'm done crying over this.*

"I'm done." Effie said it out loud, backing away from the dragoons. "I'm done with all of you." Then she pointed at her sister. "You'll be called to account for this, Vanna. When that time comes, don't expect me to use my rapport with the Lord Governor to save you from your fate."

20

VANNA

Vanna regretted her harsh words as soon as they escaped her mouth, but she could not contain them. She could not bottle them back inside the darkest corners of her soul from whence they had hatched. She watched something change in Effie as the insult struck home, felt a gulf crack open between them that she feared might never be bridged. Vanna spent the next several days apologizing, stripping the words of their power, denying their obvious truth. She blamed stress and exhaustion—and though Effie listened silently to each rationalization—the change in her sister could not be undone. Effie would never unhear the insult, even if she someday forgave.

Only one gesture remained that might thaw Effie's heart. Unfortunately, Vanna found herself in the weakest possible position to make it. With only days to go before the selection, Vanna dressed in her flight suit—collar pressed as straight as she could manage, patches of rank prominently displayed—and set out for the governor's manse.

The footman guarding the gates accepted her petition and led her into a narrow vestibule where she waited in a craftsman armchair to be summoned inside the governor's office. A few of the household conscripts moved about the interior chamber, cautiously side-eyeing Vanna and whispering back and forth. When the summons finally came, Vanna stepped carefully into the office, performed a sharp, subservient bow, and waited for an invitation to take her seat.

Ansel left her standing, suspended in uncomfortable silence as he judged her over the felt blotter on his desktop. He pointedly returned a gold fountain pen to its holster and sat back in his chair, arms folded across his barrel chest. The man's salt-and-pepper coif stood motionless atop his head, square jaw shifting as he ground his teeth.

"Sire, thank you for granting an audience on such short notice—"

Ansel cleared his throat, restoring the office to silence. A standing timepiece in the corner of the office taunted her with its swinging pendulum—back and forth, back and forth.

Ansel let Vanna linger in the silence, declining to extend an invitation for her to sit. Eventually, he spoke. "If you've come to apologize for the way you and your dragoons conducted yourselves on the Aeolus mission, I'm afraid the time for remorse is well past. You've created a substantial mess for me to clean up, and at a time when I can hardly afford the distraction."

Apologize? Vanna opened her mouth to defend herself but swallowed back the urge. She wasn't here on her own behalf and further antagonizing the governor wasn't going to help her case.

"I understand," she said, tamping down every prideful instinct threatening to surface. "It wasn't our intention to make more work for you, Sire, nor to displease our host. The rebellion on Aeolus proved more complicated than we anticipated, and we had to make quick decisions about how best to meet our mission objectives."

Ansel's stony eyes narrowed. "That's your case, is it?"

Vanna nodded. "I know our arrest of the Lord Governor was unexpected, but it seemed the only way to restore peace on Aeolus. Now the island can return to serving the interests of our host."

Ansel's inscrutable expression gave her nothing in the way of reassurance, but neither did he choose to continue the debate. "If not to grovel, then why *are* you here, Lieutenant?"

"I'm here to discuss my sister Effie, Sire." Effie's mention drew the first visible reaction from the governor—a twist of surprise and perhaps a softening in the set of his jaw, however slight. Vanna took both for signs she'd found the right trail, so she followed it. "I know she's been working among your household staff these last few weeks—tending your horses, as I understand it?" Ansel nodded. "I gather you think somewhat highly of her abilities, as I do, else you would not trust her with such an important task."

"Abilities? Yes... Your sister is a quite capable young woman." Ansel's eyes drifted a moment, and Vanna thought she saw a slight smile tweaking the corners of his lips. "She speaks too boldly by half, but she's quickwitted and pleasant—eager to learn."

"Yes," Vanna agreed. "She's all of those things...and perhaps more."

Ansel cocked one eyebrow, questioning.

Jokai fend—what would Effie say here? She'd say it's always best to be direct. "Sire, you have to understand that Effie would kill me if she knew I was here or if she heard what I was about to say, but I feel it's important for you to hear this from the person who knows her best: Her lack of Gift has been a source of tremendous shame and disappointment, and not because Effie dreams of flying with the dragoons. Effie dreams bigger than that. Bigger than anyone on Volturnus. Effie dreams of *Leviathan*. It's all she thinks about—all she's ever wanted. I wouldn't be surprised if it's the very thing that drew her to your mares—"

Ansel broke his composure at the Leviathan's mention, raising one ringed hand as he shook his head. "Lieutenant, this is hardly a discussion—"

"Sire, please!" Ansel froze again, unaccustomed to interruption of any sort. Vanna seized upon the moment's hesitation. "For years we've tested the most Gifted Zephyri across the archipelago, and *none* have demonstrated any native ability to pilot the dauphine—not since Royon successfully Ascended in the second year of the testing. I think it's time to accept that maybe we are looking in the wrong place."

Ansel grunted again, the hinted smile fallen from his angular face. Vanna thought he might dismiss her on the spot, but instead he slowly dipped his salt-and-pepper head, prompting her, "Tread carefully, Lieutenant..."

Vanna exhaled the breath she'd been holding. "I ask only that you consider my sister when making your list for the Ascension. If one Giftless Volturnian deserves the chance to test herself against the dauphine, it's Effie Strait."

Ansel drummed one thick finger against his desktop, matching the timing of his ticking clock. "Is that all, Lieutenant?"

"Yes, Sire." Vanna offered another deep bow and was dismissed.

21

EFFIE

Effie continued her work at Sire Ansel's stables as the final days before the selection slipped away from her. She didn't get another chance to speak directly with the Lord Governor, and she blamed Vanna's arrest of the Aeolian governor for occupying his time.

Vanna continued to make her effusive apologies, but Effie felt increasingly numb to her sister's words. No matter what Vanna said now, she'd spoken her heart and mind that day at the landing. With it, she'd breathed life into every ghost of self-doubt haunting Effie's Giftless existence. Vanna was no different than anyone else on Volturnus. She considered the island's Elementalists a superior breed. Effie would never be worthy in her sister's eyes, and any pitiful attempt she made to elevate her status was a nuisance at best. *Poor, Giftless Effie—the weakest strait in five generations. Willing to sell herself just to feel special.*

After the Ascension list came down, her dye would be cast. The island expected her to fall back on tradition and accept a role among the plebiscite. Unless she made a choice for herself, the village elders would see her renditioned to the fields or the knittery, married off to the first slobbering thatcher or smith eager to seed her with his equally Giftless get. Some of the village tradesmen had already begun making their insulting overtures. Akina offered to teach her the trick of spinning yak's wool into golden yarn, and Old Bolo wondered idly—in her hearing, of course—if she wouldn't find some value in tending the storm walls around the windward fields.

The indignities continued apace until selection's eve when the villagers gathered to celebrate Vernal Fete. Fete marked the beginning of the Ascension season on Volturnus. With the fields sewn and the moonberries plucked, the villagers gathered in the square to feast and dance and gossip over the Ascendant cohort's imminent reveal.

Anxious to the point of nausea, Effie didn't feel much like joining the celebration. Any other year, she might have been able to avoid the crowd, but in the year of her majority she'd be too easily missed. Her absence would only become more fodder for gossip. She could practically script the chatter herself. *Poor Giftless Effie—too ashamed to show her face at Vernal Fete. Such an entitled brat, that Effie Strait—can't even muster the dignity to show up in support of her family and friends.*

Effie would *show up*. And no matter the turmoil burning within, she was determined to project uncanny confidence and poise.

There was still hope, she reminded herself. There was still hope she'd made enough of an impression on Sire Ansel that he'd abandon tradition and append her name to the Ascension list. If that happened, all the shame and torment of the preceding weeks would vanish in a hummingwasp's heartbeat. Effie could hold her head up high and bask in the village's astonishment. She'd have defied all expectations, and in two weeks' time she'd do it again by taming a wild dauphine.

She arrived at the celebration late, an hour past sundown, while the feast was already well under way. Vanna had purchased her an expensive new Avernian gown—one of her sister's many attempted peace offerings. Effie left it untouched, draped over the back of a wooden chair in her room. Instead, she wore one of her favorite dresses with a flattering silk band accenting her narrow waist and thin straps exposing her shoulders and back. For the occasion, she'd asked one of the village seamstresses to sew new layers of colored fabric beneath the skirt and raise the hem just a few inches higher above her knee. Both alterations were designed to make a statement in the round once the dancing commenced. Effie had no intention of hiding.

She felt the eyes of nosey villagers following her as she cut a path to the dais and filled a bamboo cup with roasted root vegetables and goat stew, neither of which she had any intention of eating. She carried her head high as she worked her way down to the end of the dais and ladled herself a cup of spiced wine from the open cask. The wine she did consume. Almost immediately, she felt its fortified report lifting her spirits and steeling her nerves.

"Effie!" Vanna caught sight of her from the opposite end of the square where she was helping four dragoons lay the final planks of the dancing round. She abandoned her task, jogging over to greet her sister with a jolly, snaggle-toothed grin. "I'm so happy you decided to come."

"And why wouldn't I?" Effie countered, and there was ice in her voice even though she made sure to maintain a hostile smile for the sake of any voyeurs.

An awkward silence passed as Vanna struggled to find an answer that wouldn't offend. "I'm just glad you're here," she finally said.

"Glad to be here."

Vanna's eyes moved over Effie's outfit. "You didn't wear the gown."

"This felt more appropriate for the occasion. More *me*." Effie took a long sip of wine then hoisted her bowl of untouched food. "If you don't mind, I'm going to find somewhere to sit before the offering."

She turned her back to her sister and plodded off, careful to avoid any interactions with the other dragoons. The village had divided itself between the feasting tables, boisterous cliques of Volturnians wolfing down seconds and thirds as they descended deeper into their cups. From a table of elder craftsmen, red-faced Bolo drained his wine and belched ferociously. The dragoons threaded themselves throughout the gathering, most seated among family; those without, huddled around the edge of the dais, exchanging pleasantries and jokes. A small group of Gfitless sixteen-year-olds sat in a place of honor before the offering pit. Effie knew she'd be welcome at one of the table's dwindling seats, but she passed it by with her chin in the air. As she finished crossing the square unmolested, she clocked an empty hay bale at the edge of the gathering next to Ava, one of the village apothecaries, who looked content in her solitude and disinclined to converse.

Effie set herself down on the bale as Ava tipped the last of her stew into her wrinkled mouth and went to work on a wedge of cornbread. The old apothecary eyed her appraisingly, crumbs of cornbread still clinging to her whiskered chin.

Effie knew when she was being judged. Bristling, she set her untouched food off to the side and re-engaged with her wine cup. The two sat in uncomfortable silence as the feast carried on around them.

With the sun finally setting over the windward horizon, Theo, the thatcher's eldest son, peeled off from his table and approached Effie with a toothy smile on his wine-darkened lips. Groaning quietly, Effie straightened her posture on the hay bale to receive him.

Theo performed a stiff bow and pointed at her empty cup. "Looks like you could use a refill. May I?"

Effie batted her eyes and smiled poisonously. "Trying to get me drunk, Theo Thatcher?"

Theo blushed. "Just seems like you could use some loosening up."

"Is that how it seems?" Effie's smile didn't budge, but she did present her cup. "Your offer is accepted."

Theo exhaled with relief. His fingers glanced over Effie's hand as he accepted her cup then scampered off to the dais.

"Finally coming into your power, I see."

Surprised to hear the old apothecary speak, Effie pegged Ava with a disgruntled side-eye. "Excuse me?"

"Not all Gifts grant the power of flight." Ava's lip quirked, revealing two missing teeth as her good eye crawled Effie from head to toe. "With those legs, you'll have every nubile man in the village lining up to eat from your hand. Who needs to command the wind when you can command the hearts of men, instead?"

Effie matched Ava's smirk. "It's their hearts, is it?"

The old apothecary cackled, slapping her knee with one gnarled hand as her crooked back heaved up and down. "You know the only thing I miss about being young?"

Effie didn't know, but she assumed Ava wanted to tell her, so she asked.

"The power," Ava answered. "In my day, I had boys and men both throwing themselves over mud puddles just to keep me from soiling my skirt—not that you'd have that problem." Her eyes probed Effie's hemline.

Effie snorted with good humor. It was hard to imagine any man throwing himself in the mud just to gain this haggard crone's favor, but she supposed anything was possible.

"Of course..." Ava continued, "old age brings its own power."

Theo returned with a jolly bounce in his step. He'd filled Effie's wine cup so high that it sloshed over the brim as he bent to hand it to her.

"Sorry about that."

Effie accepted the cup, dabbing the spill with Theo's offered handkerchief.

"I was wondering..." Theo ventured. Effie folded her arms beneath her breasts, and he stuttered, clearing his throat to cover. "I was wondering if you might enjoy a dance?"

"Now?" Effie asked, glancing around at the feasting villagers and the empty round.

"No," Theo stammered. "I mean—yes, tonight—but not exactly now. After the offering. When the music starts."

Effie chewed her lower lip between two teeth, studying this thatcher. He wasn't hard on the eyes. Tall enough, though a full head shorter than Kai. Broad-shouldered and tan from his roofing work. She supposed she *did* need a partner if she was going to make a statement on the dancing round. "Ask me again. After the offering. When the music starts."

Theo's eyes lit up. He nodded, bowed again, then scampered off to rejoin his table.

Effie sipped from her wine cup and turned back to find Ava watching her with a sordid look on her face. "What?"

The old apothecary only cackled.

Golden light drained from the square as the sun slipped below the horizon. A small group of villagers bearing tinderboxes fanned across the festivities, lighting torches to cast the evening affairs in a more forgiving glow. The celebratory din quickly diminished as the doors to the roundhouse flew open.

The village elders appeared in ceremonial blue robes draped in tassels of golden yarn. Behind them, six burly men heaved against thick, fibrous ropes, pulling a wheeled cart out of the roundhouse and into the offering pit at the top of the square. On the cart lay a young golden ox of the finest breed. The elders had groomed its warm spring coat to a lustrous sheen and polished its horns so their ivory curves caught the torchlight. The beast offered nothing in the way of resistance. Effie knew the tendons in its knees had been cut, collapsing its legs so that they lay folded painfully beneath its girth.

With one final, vocal heave, the men at the ropes tipped the wagon into the center of the pit, and all eyes turned to the offering.

Effie frowned at the maimed beast. She'd always hated this part. Even as a young girl, it seemed a needless cruelty—not to mention a terrible waste. But the Volturnians had been celebrating Vernal Fete long before it came to coincide with the Celestials' Ascension. Tradition demanded they make a sacrifice to the island's Jokai after each planting to ensure a prodigious yield, and no one wanted to find out what happened when the Jokai didn't get their blood.

Ava spat on the ground at her feet. "And now the foolishness begins..." she muttered.

Effie looked over to see the same disconcerted expression on Ava that she must have sported. "What do you mean?" she whispered.

Ava gestured at the offering pit. "All this barbaric pageantry playing at mysticism. It's a performance. Nothing more."

"Not a believer, I take it?"

"I don't need belief, girl." Ava's eyes narrowed on the ring of elders collapsing around the pit. "I have knowledge."

Elder Tomon stepped forward wearing a bleached ox skull as a mask. He stood before the offering pit in his hooded robe and brandished a ceremonial machete. He flashed both broad sides of the blade as he raised it overhead, catching every flicker of torchlight on the weapon's jeweled hilt. Tomon turned the empty eyes of his mask toward the hobbled ox and began to pace the offering, running through the prayer script by rote. When he reached the front of the pit, he at last turned back to the villagers and concluded his cant.

"Jokai bless the Isles of Zephyr. Jokai bless Volturnus."

Effie parroted the valediction along with the rest of the village. Only Ava pointedly abstained. When the brief ceremony was finished, Tomon turned to the offering and raised his machete high above his head.

Effie's vision tunneled around the guileless brown eye of the ox, its lid half-closed in resignation and, perhaps, relief. The blade flashed across the offering's throat, and several villagers manning the torches threw alchemical powders into the flames. Fires flared brilliantly, shifting through alchemical tints that cast the square in flickering hues of blue, green, and red. Blood poured from the ox's open throat, splashing across the elder's robe and filling the pit.

Effie watched the ox's eye close for the final time. Its head slumped against the cart as the last of its lifeforce seeped away to prayerful cheering. Ava didn't cheer and neither did Effie.

"Performance," Ava muttered.

22

VANNA

Vanna watched Effie from a safe distance. Her sister kept her own company throughout the feast, lurking at the edge of the square next to Ava. Only hours to go before Sire Ansel rode down from his manse and unveiled the Ascension list. As the elders made their offering to the Jokai, Vanna prayed along with the rest of the villagers for a bountiful yield, but she also appended her own request that her sister's name appear on that list. It was the only thing that might break the tension between them.

With the ceremony concluded, the elders set the offering ablaze. Signaled by the light of the sacrificial pyre, a group of musicians retrieved their instruments and huddled next to the dancing round to plot out their set. Dray left the dragoons' table to join them, carrying a four-string guitar on his back where his bastard sword usually lived. Vanna overheard him noisily advocating for a bawdy drinking song to get everyone "in the mood," but the band eventually settled on an upbeat folk dance. The first notes sawed from Ludo's fiddle as the other musicians sequentially entered the fray.

A few brave dancers made their way to the round, several young dragoons among them. Vanna marked Effie still seated on a hay bale next to Ava, then scanned the square for Kendy. Her wing commander held court at a table of frequent dragoon admirers led by the knitter's daughter, Ina

Laurens. He propped one foot up on a chair and leaned over it, splashing wine from his cup as he gestured along with his tale.

Rolling her eyes, Vanna turned back to her table and found that most of her fliers had already drifted away, though one now stood before her.

Kai's sandy hair had started the night in a neat bun tied atop his head, but the leather bands had all come undone, and it now fell across his face in its usual mop. He extended one hand, innocent brown eyes probing.

"Care for a dance?"

The invitation caught Vanna off guard. She parted her lips, intending to decline, but the combination of Kai's earnest expression and wine-forged poise momentarily stole her voice. He stood statue-still in his solicitous pose, but his chest betrayed him, heart pounding visibly against its walls.

Why not? She didn't need to disappoint anybody else tonight. Vanna pressed her lips together in a sheepish smile and accepted his hand.

Kai led her to the dancing round, his head bobbing confidently above the smaller villagers around them. The other dancers parted for the Gifted pair and, when they reached the center of the round, Kai turned to her, beaming. She craned her neck to meet his gaze as they linked arms, and he began leading her through the steps of an ebullient contra.

Vanna stumbled through the first few steps, but Kai compensated gracefully, moving her body back onto the music's path with a bit of pressure on her hip or the blade of her back. Before long, the rhythm took over, and she entered a kind of musical fugue, gliding through every step and turn, eyes sweeping the dancers around them before returning to port on Kai's loamy eyes and broad-faced grin.

They traded partners, cycling through the adjacent dancers before returning to find each other as the players transitioned into a slower tune. She felt one of Kai's hands thread between her fingers while the other found her waist. She pressed her own free hand against his shoulder, surprised to find flexing braids of muscle pushing back. Part of Vanna still wanted to see Kai as that lanky boy—always chasing Effie with puppy eyes and gangly limbs that seemed too long for him to master. Until that moment, the change had been too gradual to notice. He trained harder than any of her cadets, and that training had clearly taken root in his mind as well as his form. Vanna had to accept that the Kai she knew had been replaced by this steady, confident, hard-bodied flier.

As the music picked up again, they separated, falling back into a thumping contra. Dray finally wedged his drinking song into the set, and the dancers all responded with whoops and cheers as they clapped and stomped their way through, belting the chorus along with the players.

A flash of violet hair caught Vanna's eye, momentarily breaking the musical spell. She fell out of the drinking song's rhythm as she noticed Effie at the edge of the round, trading turns with the thatcher's boy, Theo. Her sister flourished her scandalous dress as she spun, revealing sheets of color woven into the underskirt. Vanna watched her sister crane her head to the night sky, long hair whipping. Theo gawked so hard he lost the beat, but Effie seemed only peripherally aware of her clumsy partner. Several other boys in the vicinity took notice, as did a few of their fathers, each dancer peering over the shoulder of his partner to catch a glimpse of Effie Strait.

The drinking song ended, and the thrum of Dray's guitar announced the arrival of another ballad. Vanna spared one more glance for Effie as Theo fended off another young man's attempt to cut in. Theo wrapped both hands around Effie's waist possessively and pulled her against him as the other players joined the song.

Vanna considered intervening, but Kai found her and took her hand, leading her back to the center of the round. As they entered the new dance, she felt pressure from his hand drawing her body closer. She let herself be guided, stopping only once his chin nearly glanced off her head.

The proximity made both of them blush.

"Do you mind if I try something?" Kai asked.

This time, it was Vanna's heart that beat treasonously against her chest. Her body stiffened as Kai's gentle palms drew her even closer. "Depends what it is," she replied.

Kai grinned. "I think you'll like it."

He suddenly swept her in an arc across the dancing round, both his footwork and his hands guiding her into a more complicated waltz. As she followed him through the motions, she felt the kiss of wind beneath her chin, then tousling her violet bob. Kai winked at her, and the winds began to rise.

Vanna missed a step—then she lost her footing entirely. She kicked through open air and realized Kai had lifted her off the planks of the round. The two fliers levitated above the other dancers, winds twisting in a vortex around their pairing. Vanna hadn't so much as touched her Gift, but peering through her Elementalist eyes she saw the lines of force drawn up and woven in a complex skein shaped by Kai. Focus dimpled his brow, intense gaze locked on Vanna as he conducted the flow through a neat approximation of the earthbound dance, juggling their two bodies overhead.

Excited gasps rang out from the round below as the other dancers paused from their revelry to watch Kai and Vanna soaring balletically, dancing on thin air.

Kai pulled the winds tighter, drawing them close. "I think I might be ready for the corps," he whispered. "Next time you fly into enemy fire, I want to be the one watching your wing."

Vanna didn't argue.

When the song was over, he brought them both gently to the ground. The dancers around them exploded with applause.

23

EFFIE

"That was incredible."

Theo had released his strangle grip on Effie's waist and was now gawking at Vanna and Kai like every other sycophant. When they landed, Kai performed an obnoxious sweeping bow, then indicated Vanna, who responded with a blushing curtsy.

Effie waited until Theo finished his forceful applause before saying, "I think I need another drink."

"That's a great idea!" He grabbed her hand to break for the dais, but she slithered out of his grasp.

"I think I'll get this one myself."

Effie left Theo standing partnerless on the round with his hangdog expression. She really did need that drink, but she had no intention of returning to the dance. Suddenly, she didn't have the stomach for it.

Already lightheaded from spirited dancing and the wine, she filled her cup halfway and took stock of the remaining celebrants in the square. Many of the older villagers had already retired, content to wait for morning to hear which Ascendants made the governor's list. The remaining revelers were tightly clustered about the dancing round or else chatting in close-knit circles amid stacks of abandoned food. Bolo sat alone at an empty table looking ill, a wine cup still dangling from his hand.

Effie sighed. One interminable hour until Witching, the moment from which the rest of her life would unfurl like a Spurrian rug. She stared at the empty crier's post that would eventually bear the selection list until a shrill voice pierced her trance.

"You look like someone pissed in your wine."

Effie turned around to find Ava standing hunched across the dais. She spared the apothecary one indignant glance before returning to her cup.

The woman's presence felt calculated to mock her. What were the Jokai playing at, thrusting this crone in her face at every turn? Offering a glimpse of her own future, no doubt. If her expression had already been sour, Ava's arrival did nothing to sweeten its bouquet.

"I wasn't really looking for company," Effie said when Ava didn't take the hint.

Ava cocked her brow over one milky eye. "Keeping silent vigil for the selection, is it?"

"Something like that."

"Hmph." Ava turned her attention back to the distant round where the dancers had returned to circle Vanna and Kai. "Another *performance*," the old apothecary muttered, and from the way she inflected the word, Effie did not think she meant it as a compliment.

"You aren't impressed?" Effie pried.

"I'm a difficult woman to impress. I've watched generations of fliers grow up on Volturnus. They're all the same—think a little wind in their sails makes them Zephyr incarnate."

Effie snorted, and her mouthful of wine burned in her nostrils. She didn't disagree. "They are the Jokai's Gifted, though," she mused. "They're the ones the Jokai saw fit to bless with real power." *Whether they deserve it or not*, she didn't add.

"Aye, that's a truth of sorts," Ava agreed. "But it's only a partial truth, and the smallest part besides. The Jokai are a capricious kind. They don't grant blessings or heed prayers in the way most people think they do, and they certainly don't care a whit if we bleed out a strapping yak during Vernal Fete. These Elementalists we hold in such regard are only vessels. Their *power*—it's a mummer's trick. Shadows dancing on the wall and nothing more."

Effie sipped from her wine cup. She wasn't buying Ava's screed, but it still felt good to hear the dragoons and all their Gifts so pointedly dismissed. "I'd like to hear what you have to say about the Leviathan."

Ava's wrinkled mouth cracked into a gap-toothed grin. "Smart girl. The Leviathan are an entirely different matter. You haven't the time to hear my thoughts on that topic." The apothecary groaned as she stretched her hunched back to peer up at the horizon. "Almost time for the main event."

"Yes. It is." Effie suddenly felt queasy with all the wine sloshing around in her stomach.

"Given any thought to what trade you might pursue into your majority?"

"Tons," Effie said. "I'm thinking *Leviathan Pilot*."

Ava cackled, wrongly assuming it had been a joke. "If that doesn't work out for you, why don't you come around the apothecary some time and see if *real power* might suit."

With that, Ava shuffled off into the shadows beyond the dimming torchlight.

Real power? Effie shook her head, chasing the wine in her belly with the wine in her cup. *The power to mash berries into juice?* She'd sooner shrivel in the fields.

Effie stood alone as the final hour of the festival wound down. Too nervous to sit and too bitter to dance, she lingered beside the picked-over dais, her only company the boney carcass of a wild boar. At last, the players reached exhaustion and abandoned the drunken dancers pleading for "one more song." The revelers eventually accepted their fate and cleared the round.

The sixteen-year-olds began to separate, forming a disorganized mob around the crier's post. Those friends and family who'd lasted the night, gathered in a second layer, a respectful distance behind the potential Ascendants.

Hoofbeats replaced the rhythm of the music, rolling down from the hill leading out to the governor's manse. The cavalcade soon appeared: ten white mares cresting the hilltop at a casual trot. Sire Ansel struck a regal profile, leading the way atop Cloudcutter. Drawing upon the dregs of her reserves, Effie adjusted her dress and pulled back her shoulders as she stalked off to join the others. The more timid members of her cohort cleared a path, permitting her to press within view of the crier's post. Kai's sandy head stood out over the canopy of potential Ascendants. Effie diverted away from him, sidling up beside Jaffe instead. The dragoon cadet made space for her, smiling warmly with a soft cast to her eyes that Effie took for pity. She felt Kai straining overtop to try and catch her eye, but she pointedly ignored him.

Sire Ansel's herald was the first to dismount as the cavalcade approached the square. He came around to receive a parchment scroll from Ansel's saddlebag, which the governor delivered with his typical square-jawed formality. No words passed between them before the herald broke away, marching toward the crier's post.

All the excited muttering from the cohort extinguished as the herald projected his practiced voice. "Plebeian guests of Volturnus. Your Honorable Lord Governor Ansel of Brundis hereby submits these names to be tested at the Fourteenth Annual Ascension of the Zephyr Isles, a ceremony to be held seven days hence upon the arrival of the migratory dauphine to the Moonflow Lagoon on Volturnus Island. Her Lightness Kelestina of Aquilon to attend."

With that, he unfurled Ansel's scroll and, wielding a hammer and stakes, nailed the selection list top and bottom to the post.

"May the worthiest candidates Ascend," the herald concluded. He turned on his heels and marched a straight line back to the distant cavalcade. Ansel received him with a curt nod, then circled Cloudcutter to lead his honor guard back up to the manse.

The selection list stared back at the expectant cohort, its fanciful calligraphy unreadable from such a distance. Effie's own feet rooted in place, her vision tunneling around the parchment's outline.

Kai was the first to break the tension. "Well, then." A few nervous chuckles followed. "No sense in prolonging the suspense."

He broke from the pack, trudging up to the crier's post. The other dragoons followed slowly, a few steps behind, as the rest of the cohort stirred to motion. Not to be outdone, Effie forced her legs to carry her past the dragoons and up to the post at Kai's heel. She strained to read the parchment, but Kai's broad shoulders boxed her out. He ran one finger several times over the list as the pressure of their arriving cohort built behind Effie.

She saw Kai nod his head contentedly. "That's that, then." Realizing he was still blocking the list, he shuffled awkwardly out of the way, catching Effie's eye for a fleeting second as she pushed past him to read the names for herself.

Bodies elbowed and shoved for a better view, but Effie felt nothing, heard only the hollow sound of her own breathing and the blood thrumming in her ears.

Five lines of calligraphy adorned the list. Five names. *Half* the number Volturnus submitted just one year prior. Her lips moved as she read them.

Jaffe Feor...

Seulin Rai...

Kai Bowker...

Lya Song...

...and Min Baris.

Effie read the names again, her heart sinking into her stomach. She read them over and over, hoping to find some hidden line of text where none existed.

Jaffe.

Seulin.

Kai.

Lya.

And *Min*.

She felt herself shrinking away from the post, ushered backward as others stepped forward to receive the same dire report.

Five names. Five Ascendants. And Effie was not one of them.

No surprises, then.

As dictated by tradition, Sire Ansel had picked the only five Elementalists on Volturnus in the year of their majority. Effie felt the heat rising in her cheeks, suddenly ashamed to have worn her yearning so prominently—abashed she even had the audacity to believe it would turn out any other way.

She drifted away from the cohort, now thronging around the five dragoons to offer congratulations and humble words of support. No one else seemed to share her disappointment. Effie Strait was the only Giftless girl on Volturnus foolish enough to think she might actually be picked.

Tears began to burn in the corners of her eyes as Vanna found her.

"No..." Vanna said.

No tears, Effie reminded herself. *I said I was done crying over this.* Effie looked up at her sister, expecting to find some patronizing flavor of pity. Rage flashed across her sister's expression, instead. The dam of Effie's stubborn mantra no longer held, and she broke down. Her sister pulled her into a tight embrace and let her weep against her shoulder. She hadn't wept like this since she was two years old, watching Vanna collapse inward at the fell tidings of their parents' demise.

"I wasn't picked," Effie cried.

Vanna hushed softly, her fingers threading Effie's long hair. The sisters held each other until the sobbing subsided.

Effie expected condolences, but Vanna only muttered, "This isn't right."

Effie shook her head. "It is, though," she said. "I'm *not* an Elementalist, and I'll never bond a Leviathan. I'm not worthy."

Vanna snarled at that, her snaggletooth displayed like the fang of some feral beast. "There's something I need to do," she said. "I'll meet you back at the cottage."

24

VANNA

Vanna almost screamed as she broke away from her devastated sister and drew upon her Gift to soar past the crier's post. Her arcing trajectory carried her along the path to Ansel's manse.

She landed in front of the cavalcade with a blast of dirt and gravel that forced the governor to rear his prized mare.

"Lieutenant Strait!" he shouted over the sound of his mount's startled whinny. "What do you think you're doing?"

Vanna jabbed her finger up at the mounted governor. "You left her off!"

Cloudcutter snorted and pulled at her reins. Ansel's thick eyebrows knit together across his reddening brow as he settled his jumpy mare. Once his horse had calmed, he shot Vanna a contemptuous glare. "What are you on about, girl?"

"Effie!" Vanna shouted. "I thought we had an understanding."

"An *understanding*?" His eyes bugged from his square head.

"Yes!" Vanna's hands trembled with rage. She balled them into fists. "We both agreed that Effie was *special*—that she deserved a chance to Ascend!"

"Don't be ridiculous," Ansel spat. "I said no such thing. The Ascension is a ceremony for the *Gifted*. You can hardly expect our host to waste her valuable time watching mundane plebs attempt to *mount* a wild Leviathan. It simply isn't done."

The disdain in Ansel's voice set Vanna's blood to boil. Without intending it, she drew upon her Gift. Her feet left the ground, and she rose up on summoned wind, drawing face-to-face with the governor atop his mount.

He withdrew his head. A moment of real fear flashed across his Patrician expression, and Vanna used it to press her position. "You need to fix this! Post an amendment!"

"This list is already delivered to Aquilon," he snarled. "It's done." When Vanna didn't withdraw, Ansel lowered his voice. "Stand down, Lieutenant."

Vanna didn't stand down. "You're making a mistake."

Ansel flashed his pearly teeth. He whispered something inaudible, and his mare suddenly reared on her hind-legs, forelimbs kicking. Two steel-shoed hooves cracked Vanna across the chest, shattering her concentration and slamming her painfully to the ground.

Vanna gasped in a fetal ball, chest screaming with every stuttering intake of breath. She heard Cloudcutter snort as Ansel stirred her back to motion, slowing as he passed.

"Don't worry, Lieutenant." The governor's arrogant Patrician voice had been restored. "I won't hold your intemperance against your sister. You're right about one thing. Effie *is* special. I intend to conscript her for service among my household staff."

No! She would have screamed it, if she only had her breath.

"Once the Ascension is over, she'll be summoned to the manse to be outfitted. I expect she'll look quite fetching in gray and brass." Cloudcutter's hooves kicked clouds of dust over Vanna's crumpled form.

"Who knows?" Ansel's voice drifted as he continued down the path. "In a few years and with a bit more meat on her bones, she might even earn an honored place warming my bed. We'll have to see how inclined she is to courtesy. Though, reluctant partners aren't without their pleasures, I suppose. We'll find plenty of uses for her in the meantime."

No... Vanna rolled over, still gasping.

Hoofbeats taunted her, receding down the path.

Effie...

25

EFFIE

Effie waited up for Vanna until the wine and her empty stomach conspired to turn on her, summoning a headache that throbbed behind her eyes. Surrendering to the repercussions of her excesses, she retired to endure a night of fitful sleep.

Leviathan visited her dreams, as they so often did, but in between bouts of tossing wakefulness, she found their oneiric dispositions less inclined than usual. In one vibrant scene, she stood atop Widow's Peak with a pod of dauphine circling overhead, their pink and blue flukes churning up the air around her. The sky became so livid with their commotion that she struggled to catch her breath. She tried to force her will upon the wild creatures, pleading with them to descend—to settle and permit her to mount. The dauphine ignored her every overture, taunting her with their cackling song as a black shadow unfurled across the dreamscape. Effie squinted into the sudden darkness as the dauphine scattered, fleeing the descending wings of Devil Ray. Maug's sharp blue eyes found her from the skate's iron deck. His scarred face broke into an evil grin as he ordered a cannon assault. Projectiles struck the promontory, and Effie awoke in a cold sweat.

Panting, she checked her bedroom window where the season's early falselight greeted her with an anemic pre-dawn glow. Still groggy from the wine, she momentarily forgot the evening's disappointment, but reality awaited in the waking world.

It was all over. Sire Ansel had delivered his list. Effie hadn't been chosen.

She heard the door to the cottage creek open and shut, followed by the sound of Vanna's feet shuffling across the kitchen floor. *So late.* Effie contemplated rolling back over and braving her dreamscape, but curiosity got the better of her. She crept out of her room to see what her sister had been about in the wee hours of the night.

She found Vanna hunched over the table, bandages wrapped around her shoulder and chest. Suddenly alert, Effie ran to her side. "What happened to you?"

Vanna looked up. "I'm sorry—did I wake you?"

"I was already up," Effie said. Vanna grimaced as Effie helped her into a chair. "*Jokai fend*—who did this to you?"

"Effie..."

"No, Vanna. I want to know where you've been. It's nearly dawn."

Vanna sighed. "Will you set the tea, at least?"

Frowning, Effie placed the kettle to boil and rummaged two mugs from the cupboard. She sat next to her sister with the empty mugs in hand. "Talk."

"I went to confront Sire Ansel about the list," Vanna said.

"You *what?*" Effie didn't know what she expected her sister to say, but it wasn't that. "Why would you do that?"

Vanna shifted on her chair, wincing from the pain in her chest. "You deserved to be on the list, Eff. It isn't right that you shouldn't get your chance to tame the dauphine."

"And he attacked you?"

"Not exactly," Vanna said. "I might have startled his mare."

For once, Effie was speechless. The kettle started whistling, and she retrieved it to pour the tea. They both sat in silence in front of their steaming mugs until Effie finally muttered, "You didn't have to do that..."

"Yes, I did," Vanna said. She reached across the table and clasped Effie's hand. "I'd do anything for you, Eff."

Effie felt her sister's clammy hand threading calloused fingers between her own. "I know..." she whispered, squeezing back.

"You do?" Now Vanna sounded like the one on the verge of tears.

Effie nodded, squeezing her sister's hand again. "I've been awful to you..." she admitted.

"No worse than I deserved." Vanna sniffed and ventured a sip of her tea. "I didn't mean what I said that day on the landing, you know. You *are* special, Eff." Then her voice turned sour. "And you're nobody's whore."

Effie stared into her mug. Every previous iteration of this same apology had rolled off her like raindrops on an oilcloak. Not this one, though. This one soaked her straight through. Vanna *wasn't* like everyone else on Volturnus. She alone saw Effie's worth, whether she was Gifted or not. She believed in it so strongly that she actually confronted a Patrician. It tore at Effie's heart to think she might never get to pilot a Leviathan, but she felt some of the sting from that loss subsiding. Her sister's earnest admiration proved a potent balm.

Effie released Vanna's hand and ran her fingers gently along the strap of bandages harnessed over her shoulder. "How bad is it?"

"This?" Vanna's lips quirked in an almost-grin. "Just bruises, thankfully. The menders don't think I broke any ribs. I'll be grounded for a time, though."

"Island-bound like the rest of us mere mortals, eh?"

Vanna laughed, then grimaced. "Ow. If you could keep the humor to a minimum until I'm healed, that would be greatly appreciated."

Effie finally sipped her tea, which had already begun to cool.

"I am sorry," Vanna said. "I know how much you wanted this."

Effie nodded thoughtfully.

She *did* want this. Nothing meaningful had changed. Nothing *real*... Vanna's sentiment rang true enough, but the condolences seemed suddenly premature. Her sister's gesture of confidence reawakened something inside of her—a spark of perseverance the night's humiliation had nearly snuffed out. That spark had carried her through every day since she first accepted her Giftless fate—every day since Kai manifested, if she was being honest with herself. Tonight's failure was a truth of a kind, but in Ava's words, it was only a partial truth and the smallest part, besides.

The selection list held no power over her; it was only ink and paper and nothing more. Sire Ansel was a powerful man, but his authority didn't extend to Effie's dreams. She was born to pilot Leviathan. No man— plebeian or Patrician—had the power to keep her from that destiny.

"Who said it's over?" Effie mused.

Vanna sat back, squinting. "What are you plotting?"

"No plots," Effie lied. "Vernal Fete is over, and the list has been read. I'm going to do what's expected of any Volturnian entering her majority."

Vanna looked skeptical. "And what's that?"

Effie sipped her tea to conceal a mad grin. "I'm going to get a job."

26

EFFIE

Effie sent Vanna to convalesce in bed and finished her tea, waiting for sunrise as her latest plot took shape in her mind. With new light dappling the cottage through a leeward window and birdsong lilting beyond, she dressed and set out for the apothecary shop at the village's edge.

She found the shop's front door ajar. Bells jingled as she pushed her way in. The storefront smelled musty and acrid from the outgassing of alchemical reagents lining the walls in glass beakers and tinted flasks. It looked like it hadn't been swept in a month. Two of Ava's middle-aged apprentices were already at work, busying themselves behind the counter arranging fresh tonics and ointments on display cases to advertise their sale. One of them, a plump woman with her hair tied in one long chestnut braid, startled at the sound of Effie's arrival, nearly dropping the stoppered flask in her hand.

"*Jokai fend*—" She pressed one hand to her aproned chest. "Can I help you? We don't open for another hour."

The second apprentice continued her work unperturbed as Effie approached the counter.

"I apologize for the early call," she said, "but I'm not here to shop. I spoke with Ava during last night's Fete. She invited me in to learn more about your work."

The plump apothecary set her flask down on the counter and pursed her lips. "Did she now?"

Before Effie could answer, Ava's muffled voice crept out from the back chamber. "Who's out there, Reddy? If it's Geno again, tell him those sores on his rump can wait until we're open."

Effie stifled a laugh as Leddy scowled then disappeared into the back room. She heard more muffled discussion that she couldn't quite make out, then an overlong silence before Ava appeared behind the counter in Leddy's place.

Ava planted her tongue in her whiskered cheek, milky eye probing.

Effie had expected a more gracious reception. The old apothecary had been awfully solicitous at Fete. "Hello, Ava." She curtsied, affecting a pleasant smile. "I'm here to take you up on last night's offer."

"I figured as much," Ava replied, suspicion still burning through her milky eye. "What changed?"

"I'm not sure what you mean—"

"Of course you are!" Ava threw her gnarled hands in the air. "I'm half-blind, girl—not deaf. A few hours ago, you sounded less than enthusiastic about the prospect of learning our trade."

Effie shook her head. "I think you might have misinterpreted—"

"I'm not dumb, either," Ava spat.

Jokai fend—no sense performing for this one. Effie dropped the fake smile and stomped up to the counter. "In case you didn't notice, the Ascension list was rather short this year."

"Bah—I pay little attention to such trifles."

"Then let me summarize the important bit for you. It doesn't look like I'll be piloting Leviathan, after all."

Ava's wrinkled lips began to curl. Effie stared into her half-blind eyes until she broke into one of her fits of maniacal cackling. "I knew I read you right. What were you thinking, flouncing in here all curtsies and ingratiating smiles? I'll have no more of that nonsense in this shop."

"Works just fine for me," Effie said.

Ava cackled again, then shuffled around the counter to get a better look at Effie. She grabbed her arms and squeezed with surprising strength. "All that talk of power got you piqued, didn't it?

"Something like that."

Ava squeezed her arms again before releasing her. She stood back, stroking a single white whisker extending from a wart on her chin. "So, you think you might be interested in learning the craft?"

"I don't know," Effie answered honestly. "I think I want to know more before I make any decisions."

Ava nodded. "Savvy enough. The craft isn't a good fit for fickle minds or changeable hearts. It takes decades to master." She gestured at the thinner of her two apprentices still stocking vials behind the display case. "Nadia's been an apprentice going on twenty years."

"Twenty-one years this midwinter," Nadia added without looking up from her task.

"Longer than you've been alive," Ava said. "You think you've got the grit for such a long term of indenture?"

"Honestly?" Effie asked.

"No—lyingly," Ava spat. "Of course, *honestly*, girl. If you're going to keep wasting time with stupid questions your apprenticeship will stretch on to eternity."

"*Honestly*," Effie emphasized, "I don't know if I'm a fit. But like I said, I want to learn more."

Ava plucked at her whisker again, then turned her head toward the back room, milky eye still fixed on Effie. "Leddy—you going to have that admixture finished before the Dire Night?"

"Only if Nadia covers my shifts at the shop," Leddy's muffled voice returned.

Ava nodded to herself.

"What's the admixture?" Effie asked.

Effie caught a glint of excitement in the apothecary's clouded lens. "You want to get a feel for the craft? Next Dire Night's in two days. Meet me at the back of the shop one hour past dawn and not a minute late. And wear some pants, for once. There won't be anyone for you to impress with those stems you're so proud of."

Effie returned to the apothecary promptly, as instructed. In the two days since her first visit, the early delegations from the other islands began to trickle onto Volturnus. Nimbion and Avernus each sent small fleets of kite-ships, each one packed with spectators and chaperones accompanying their Ascendants. The Avernians brought word of a contracted zeppelin en route from Aeolus, destined to make landfall in two days' time. Any other year, Effie would have spent her time eagerly scouting the new arrivals. She and Kai used to make a game of guessing the Ascendants at a glance. She hadn't the time for such foolishness now. Not with the success of her half-baked plan still balanced on the edge of a butcher's blade.

On the morning of the Dire Night, heavy clouds occluded the dawn's light, shrouding the early morning in near-darkness and threatening rain. She found Ava behind the apothecary shop, guarding a yakcart laden with unlabeled jugs of some rich, purple tincture. Leddy and Nadia shuttled back and forth between the cart and the back of the shop, stacking the final jugs until the cart's wheels began to sink under its burden.

Ava greeted Effie's arrival with a curt nod. "On time. That's a fine start."

Effie watched Nadia testing the yakcart's yokes and tightening the harnesses around the four golden yaks set to pull its weight. "Are we going somewhere?" Effie asked.

"What did I say about stupid questions, girl?"

Effie bit down on her lip, swallowing her irritation. "*Where* are we going?" she corrected.

"The Green Maw," Ava replied.

Effie gaped at her then slammed her mouth shut, though she was certain Ava noticed. The old crone wasn't half as blind as she let on. The Green Maw was a small span of untamed jungle at the south end of Volturnus, beyond the farthest of the village's outlying fields. The early farmers who first broke the land stopped short of its boundaries, leaving the Maw to wild. The jungle remained as it had always been—undisturbed and infrequently visited. A superstitious taboo warned the Volturnians from breaching its geas, and apocryphal accounts of its disruption featured prominently in several of the island's cautionary tales.

"You're sure she's ready for this?" Nadia asked, finishing her task with the final yak. "You don't want to scare her off so soon."

"Bah!" Ava waved dismissively as she hobbled forward and reached for the cart's first step. Leddy sprang forth to assist her into the saddle. "You don't scare so easily, do you girl?"

"I don't think so. No." Effie circled the cart, eyeing the unmarked jugs as she passed. "What are we hauling?"

Ava and Nadia locked eyes in some unspoken exchange.

"Moonberry juice," Ava said.

Effie turned back to the jugs with newfound reverence. This cart must have held an entire season's yield—so much value in one unguarded place! The apothecaries typically kept their Nectar in a heavy safe buried within the stone foundation of their shop. Only Ava and Sire Ansel held the key. How easy it would be for one jug to disappear from an open cart behind the back of an allegedly half-blind crone...

"The admixture is only a precursor to Nectar," Ava said—an uncanny response, considering the content of Effie's private musings. "It's inert until we finish working our craft, so don't get any hair-brained ideas. Come on." She patted the passenger seat next to her own. "Time's a-wasting."

With one last glance at the priceless jugs, Effie mounted the cart.

Ava held the reins in her crooked hands as the cart trundled down the road out of town and onto the farmways running south from the village. Effie inhaled the sweet scent of fresh-turned loam as they rode past newly planted rows stretching beyond the horizon.

"Not as talkative as I assumed," Ava finally said. "Don't you have any questions?"

"Plenty," Effie said. "I'm just not sure if they're the right ones yet."

Ava cackled and cracked the reins. "I'll start, then. Planning to wed anytime soon? Do you want children? If so, how many?"

The personal questions caught Effie off guard, and she found she didn't really have an answer. She knew how many Volturnian girls dreamt of marriage and starting a family, and she'd be lying if she said she hadn't considered it—hadn't formed a few blurry notions when she let herself stare too long at Kai. Errant daydreams aside, husbands and children didn't factor heavily in Effie's plans for her life, but neither did she want to preclude the possibility.

"I saw the way you were dancing with that thatcher's boy at Fete," Ava prodded.

Effie let the insinuation slide. "Is it even allowed?" she asked instead. "If I were to become an apothecary, would I be permitted to marry? To bear children?"

"Why the hell not?" Ava spat over the side of the cart. "Just because I never let any of my many suitors seed me with their squirming get doesn't mean it's forbidden. Nadia has three little brats of her own, and let me tell you—watching her has only fortified my decision."

"That's good to know... I guess."

"I'm only interested in what sort of demands on your time I'm potentially contending with. The craft requires commitment. So do children. So do husbands, come to think of it. Maybe them most of all." Ava laughed at her own joke.

Effie didn't much care for the direction of this conversation, so she elected to change the subject. "When you say 'the craft,' you mean the apothecary, no?"

"You'll find I mean what I say." Ava's lips worked as she moistened her wrinkled mouth. "The apothecary's just a shop. The craft is the name we use to refer to our *trade*."

"Could you be more specific?"

Ava didn't answer right away. She first craned her neck to check the position of the sun still cresting over the leeward horizon. "The craft and the people who practice it have gone by many names," she finally said. "We've been called mystics, shamans, soothsayers, skaldi, cielomancers... *witches*. Our trade is as old as Volturnus itself—as old as the skies of Ciel and just as infinite. We are the *seekers*—the wise ones who read the leylines of the Jokai and learn to speak their silent tongue. When I talk of *real power*, girl, that's what I mean."

Effie turned her head, hoping Ava wouldn't clock her incredulous expression. She didn't know how much of the crone's numinous ramblings she believed. It all sounded awfully high and mighty for a group of women selling potions and blister balm over a counter at the edge of town. Despite her skepticism, she couldn't deny that Ava had her piqued.

The tightly clustered farm plots thinned as their cart drew closer to the boundary of the Green Maw. As they passed the final acres of orchard, another question popped into Effie's head.

"Why are all the apothecaries women?" she asked. "Is that a rule?"

Ava spared her an amused look before returning her eyes to the dirt road ahead. "Not a rule, exactly. No. I've seen a few men take to the craft in my day, but most don't have the proclivity."

"What does that mean?"

Ava considered her answer for a moment before replying. "The Jokai are tricksters. It takes a special kind to master their ways. To learn the craft, you need to be hard as stone and soft as down. You have to be steadfast and compromising, logical and obtuse. You need to be just and capricious, merciful and cruel. To work the craft, you need to lie truthfully. You need to be honest and false, mysterious and bare. You need to bend in half without breaking. How many men do you know capable of containing so many contradictions?"

Effie wasn't sure she knew *anyone* like Ava described. She wasn't sure the crone's addled speeches even made any practical sense.

They passed the final orchard before midday, and the jungle's lips parted to swallow them like a maw in truth. A cart path continued past the line of untamed trees, a surprise to Effie. "Who maintains this trail?" she asked.

Ava snorted. "You will. If I accept you as my apprentice, that is."

They trundled on, serenaded by the fluting sound of birdsong and the distant grunts of hidden beasts. As they pushed deeper inside the jungle, Ava suddenly pulled up on the reins and drew the yaks to a groaning stop. Her nose wrinkled as she sniffed the air.

"You smell that?"

Effie drew a deep draught of damp jungle air. "It smells like a campfire," she said.

"Do you see any smoke?" Ava asked.

Effie looked around. She didn't, but the dense foliage obscured most of her potential lines of sight. She shook her head.

"Old then..." Ava muttered to herself.

A distant rustling in the trees drew Effie's attention. She glanced up through a break in the canopy and saw the profile of a hawk soaring over-head at incredible altitude. The hawk banked on its massive wings and disappeared beyond a dense line of trees.

"What is it?" Ava hissed.

"It's just a bird," Effie told her.

Ava's frown added two deep grooves to her wrinkled chin. "Best we get on with our task." She cracked the reins, stirring the yaks back to motion. "We're nearly there."

The wide trail ended in a clearing centered around a deep ditch lined with some kind of fibrous netting. Effie helped Ava out of the cart and the two walked over to peer into the pit. Plenty of questions swirled in Effie's mind, but none of them seemed useful enough to suit Ava, so she kept her mouth shut.

"Time to unload." Ava left Effie staring into the pit and hobbled back to the cart to hoist one of the jugs of moonberry juice. "Don't just stand there goggling. Many hands make light work. Come on."

Effie skipped over and grabbed her own jug, then followed Ava to the pit and watched her dump out its precious contents. Stifling another round of pointless questions, she followed suit, cycling back and forth between the oxcart and the pit until the last jug had been emptied.

Ava braced her back, groaning, as they both stared into the pit now brimming with purple juice.

"You've gone quiet again," Ava said.

"I'm not sure what to ask," Effie admitted.

"In that case, silence will do." Ava retrieved a leather satchel from the back of the cart and handed Effie a small jar of ointment and a strip of gauze. She returned to the satchel and produced a curved knife that looked like it had seen plenty of use. The blade flashed. Effie gasped as the old apothecary drew its sharp curve across the palm of her hand.

Ava balled her fist around the gash and held it steady over the open pit. Effie watched her squeeze twelve precise drops of blood into the moonberry juice before withdrawing the hand and indicating the gauze. "Wrap me up, will you? I'm not as fortified against infection as I used to be."

Effie did as she was told, spreading a thin layer of balm over the gash and wrapping it tightly with the sterile gauze.

Ava nodded approvingly at the ministrations. "Time to go," she said.

"You're just going to leave the island's entire moonberry harvest in a pit in the middle of the jungle?"

Ava nodded. "The island's Jokai need time to work their charms, and they don't like an audience. It should only take the night. I'll send Nadia and Leddy back here tomorrow to confirm the transmutation and retrieve the Nectar if it's done."

Effie's eyes crawled over the brimming pit. Tendrils of Ava's blood squirmed across its surface, slowly beginning to mix. "I thought you said the Jokai didn't care a whit for blood?"

"I said they don't care a whit for *yak's blood*, girl. Their appetites are more refined than that." Ava turned to her then, and Effie saw her own face reflected to chilling effect in the old woman's milky eye. "Vernal Fete is as old as the island itself. The offering wasn't always a performance, and it didn't used to be half as genteel."

27

EFFIE

"An apothecary? Really, Eff?" Vanna looked incredulous.

"I'm just exploring my options." Effie quickly bussed her sister's dishes and deposited them into the wash basin. Vanna rose to help her, but her bruises forced her back into her seat. "I do admit," Effie continued as she began to scrub the crusty plate, "the work's more tiring than I expected. I think I'll turn in early." She finished cleaning the plate then turned to her sister, still perched against the basin. "You should do the same if you're ever going to heal."

"Yes, mom," Vanna grumbled.

Effie helped her rise from the chair and ushered her into her bedroom. "I don't want to see your face until the sun's up."

Vanna grumbled again, but she didn't resist. She lowered herself gingerly onto her feather mattress as Effie pulled the door shut behind her. Vanna did need her rest to recover, but Effie also needed her sister out of the way and why couldn't both things be true at once? She retired to her own room and lay awake atop her quilt, waiting for the hours to tick by as she quietly pretended to sleep.

So much of her day spent with Ava in the Green Maw unsettled her. She'd been quick to dismiss the crone's wild ramblings, but some of the sentiments still swirled through her thoughts. The old apothecary described the Jokai as "tricksters." To master their ways, one needed to be hard as stone and soft as down; merciful and cruel; true and false. Effie didn't know what to make of it, but fortunately she wouldn't have to figure it out.

Effie Strait had no intention of learning Ava's "craft."

Effie waited until she was certain Vanna was fast asleep, then she slipped into her boots and crept out of her room, gently closing the creaking door behind her. With light fingers, she picked through the crate of detritus stored at the bottom of the kitchen closet until she found one of Vanna's old alchemical torches—the kind the dragoons used during night patrol. She confirmed that the torch still worked, checked her sister's door one last time for good measure, then forged out into the night.

The Dire Night only occurred three times a year, when both new moons coincided. The pitch black of the celestial occasion afforded Effie all the cover she needed to creep out of the sleeping village unseen and begin the long southward crossing to the Green Maw.

She kept the torch extinguished until she was out among the sparsely populated fields. Shadows summoned by the alchemical light twisted on the periphery, but Effie kept her focus on the road ahead, ignoring every unsettling shape and sound. Without a cart, it took her half the night just to reach the jungle's boundary. The deeper darkness beyond and her own ingrained fear of the taboo warned her against this trespass, but she'd already come too far to turn around. She would not return to the village empty-handed. Mustering her courage with a stuttering breath, she breached the boundary and continued down the apothecaries' cart path.

Nocturnal life hounded her passage with chittering. More than once, Effie flashed her torch off the path only to catch a retreating tale or the rustling of brush. Muttering impotent prayers for the Jokai's protection, she forged onward, carefully keeping to the outlines of the path. How easy it would be to lose herself in the jungle's perfect dark. She hardly trusted her wayfinding skills to lead her back if she lost the path. The sooner she reached the clearing, the sooner she could return to the safety of the village and her feather bed.

Another hour passed as Effie penetrated deeper into the Maw's forbidden depths. Eventually, she reached the pit where she and Ava deposited the moonberry harvest. The gibbering and patter of the jungle's hidden beasts fell away, and an unnatural silence gripped the clearing. As she approached the pit, Effie heard only the sound of leaves and sticks crunching beneath her feet. A chill breeze raised the fine hairs on the back of her neck, and she prickled with the sense of unseen eyes marking her trespass.

The sensation grew so unsettling that Effie stopped her approach to scan the edges of the clearing with her torch. Seeing nothing, she proceeded, though the feeling of being watched only intensified with every step. She swept her torch around the clearing once more and stopped over a purple clutch of serrated brush.

The leaves parted, opening their sharp skein around the black outline of an oblong head.

Effie held her torch and her breath as a tower of eyes opened along the head. The eyes blinked as one—two rows of five and an eleventh centered at the apex. With a gasp, Effie quickly extinguished her torch, but the eyes remained, glowing with their own endemic light.

Brush rustled as the rest of the creature revealed itself, rising out of the thicket on two gray legs.

The creature had the long face of a baboon, with a hairless snout and blue pigments cushioning its tower of eyes. It hunched its primate back as it approached, bipedal gait nearly human, long arms bent at its sides. Effie quickly attempted to reignite her torch, but the trinket failed her, leaving her own eyes at the mercy of the creature's glow. She cursed under her breath as thick, primate lips curled back, exposing four long fangs at the corners of its jaws.

To Effie's horror, the creature spoke, its voice rich and resonant—impossibly deep. "What find we here but a mouse in the cave, come to contest the lion's meal."

Instinct pleaded with Effie to turn and run. Smelling her fear, the creature rooted her feet to the ground with a sonorous growl that shook the canopy overhead.

"Ah-ah," it said. "The time for retreat only *precedes* the moment of capture. *Tresspasserrrrr.*"

"Trespasser?" Effie squeaked, sounding too like the mouse of this creature's accusation.

All eleven eyes stacked across its hairless face blinked. "It would prefer we name it *thief*? Such is its intent, though yet unfulfilled. We are generous in our naming. Yesss."

Effie stared into the creature's many eyes, beautiful and terrible, and in their depths, she discovered with what—or with *whom*—she spoke. "You're a Jokai," she muttered, awe and a sense of the sublime restoring momentary calm.

The Jokai bent its head in confirmation. "And you're a greedy little mouse caught traipsing where you shouldn't. What would you have us do?"

Effie breathed in. "Since you're asking, I'd have you leave me to accomplish what I came for."

The Jokai's gibbering laughter reawakened the urge to run. "And why should we do that?"

"Because you *owe* it!" The words bubbled out of Effie unbidden. Fear pushed her down into a deep well of grievance, and she suddenly resented the creature's threats.

"Tell us, then," the Jokai coaxed. "Tell us what the lion owes the mouse."

"Your kind denied me my birthright," she said. "I'm here to take it for myself."

Another fanged smile. The Jokai suddenly vanished and reappeared on the opposite side of the pit. In the creature's endemic glow, she saw every curve of its bare pectorals and sharp, guttered abs. On its hind-legs it stood nearly seven feet tall. It stared down at Effie with nothing but a few paces of ground between them. Its pink tongue swept the curve of its mouth.

Effie knew when something was trying to intimidate her. Already well beyond terror, she met the creature's sudden proximity with defiance. Squinting into its eyes, she took a step forward. "Your kind are supposed to protect the people—"

The Jokai unleashed another violent growl. Effie reflexively shielded herself from its wind—nearly gagged from the carrion scent of its breath. "We protect the *island*, mouse." Its voice surrounded her, arriving from every angle of the jungle.

"Then we want the same thing!" Effie shouted. "But I can't help protect the island if no one recognizes my Gift. *That's* why I came here tonight."

The Jokai lowered itself onto its long forelimbs so that the two of them stood eye-to-eye. Pink nostrils flared as it sniffed. "You smell frightened."

"Yes."

"Then you are as wise as you are foolish." The gibbering laughter returned. "A little mouse come to right a wrong as measured by its own ambition. We are not so blind to its heart. Even the lion would not begrudge the mouse its boldness."

"If you can see my heart," Effie ventured, "then you know you'll have to kill me to stop me from leaving with what I came for."

The Jokai exposed its bottom fangs. "We do not take without an equal exchange..." it mused. "But nor do we *offer*. We would pay for its life if we must, but perhaps an exchange would better suit? You've come such a long way, and we speak not only of tonight."

"What sort of exchange are you proposing?"

"Ah-ah, little mouse." The Jokai rose up on its hindlegs again and extended one finger, wagging it back and forth. "Services to be named later."

"You want me to agree to an open-ended exchange?" Ava's sermon echoed in the back of Effie's mind: *The Jokai are tricksters.*

The Jokai nodded. "Like for like. You live in what is and we deal in what will be. What will be from our exchange will set the terms of repayment."

Effie saw the Jokai's riddle for the trap that it was, but what choice did she have? If she denied it, perhaps this creature would let her leave the jungle empty-handed to continue on with her mundane life, but that life was worth little and less to her. Effie came here to take her fate back into her own hands, and if that meant selling a piece of that fate to this Jokai, then at least it was hers to sell.

"I accept," Effie said.

The Jokai's fanged smile returned. Effie expected some ritual to sanctify the exchange, but the creature vanished again and reappeared at the edge of the pit with its back to her. Its naked rump glowed as it squatted over the moonberry juice. She heard the trickle of water as the Jokai began urinating into the pool. Effie scowled, repulsed, as the creature finished making its contribution with an obscene shiver and shake.

Its sonorous voice returned from every angle of the jungle. "We do not bless or curse, little mouse. Our only Gift is *choice*. You are but a bundle of passages—both taken and denied."

The Jokai straightened its back, then vanished with a gust of wind and a distant rustle of brush.

Effie shivered in the sudden silence and the restoration of the jungle's perfect dark. She checked her torch again and found its light returned to function.

A cautious part of her screamed to turn back—to take nothing that this Jokai offered and assume no debt in return. Effie gave it no heed. If the Jokai's only blessing was choice, then she'd made hers long ago.

She approached the pool of moonberry juice befouled by Ava's blood and the Jokai's urine. She pulled a small, stoppered flask from her cloak and bent to steal a dram.

Effie returned to the village with only minutes to spare before dawn. Janus the barkeep spotted her while she was out clearing the evening's trash. Effie felt the barkeep's suspicious gaze following her down the path to her cottage, but thankfully the woman didn't deign to intervene.

She found the cottage dark. Vanna still slept in her room, door shut as Effie had left it. Effie crept quietly into her own bedroom and changed out of her traveling clothes before tucking herself in. Beneath the sheets, she cradled the small flask of pilfered Nectar.

The purple juice looked much like it had on the back of Ava's cart, though it now glowed with the same endemic light she'd seen around the Jokai.

The details of her exchange with the creature grew foggy as she drifted toward sleep, like the outlines of some half-remembered dream. She tried to replay the conversation—to recall the words that passed between them and the terms of their half-made deal. The harder she probed these details, the more they slipped through her grasp like so much sand in a sieve. With dawn light seeping into her bedroom, she began to question whether the chance encounter had happened at all.

Her eyelids grew heavy, and she finally drifted off to sleep. The only evidence of her adventure, the steady ache in her blistered feet and the stolen vial clasped between her hands.

28

VANNA

The final days before the Ascension crawled by for Vanna, so unaccustomed to all the free time without drills and patrols to attend. She attempted to rejoin her cadets once she regained enough strength to hike out to the landing, but Kendy wouldn't hear it. He sent her home to recuperate, scolding her. "I need you healed, not wincing through drills."

He was almost as bad as Effie.

Volturnus bustled with new arrivals, but the cottage felt lonely. Effie continued to make herself scarce. She spent most of her time outside the house or else holed up in her room with the door closed. Vanna assumed she was still working with the apothecaries—"exploring her options," as she put it. Vanna tried to picture her sister enduring a long, cerebral apprenticeship with Ava, but the costume didn't fit. Skepticism aside, she couldn't deny that Effie had regained some of her confidence. She seemed more determined than she had in weeks. Not happy, exactly, but *focused*—and if working with Ava kept Effie away from Sire Ansel, that was all to the good.

Vanna still couldn't shake the intuition that her sister was up to something. The tension between them had all but evaporated since Vernal Fete, and Vanna was hesitant to attempt any line of questioning that might shake the foundation of their unsteady peace. Whatever Effie was plotting, she'd just have to let it play out and—if necessary—help her sister deal with the consequences.

On the morning of Ascension Day, Vanna dressed in her dragoon uniform and brushed out her violet hair. She still couldn't fly, but the pain in her chest had abated enough that a long march wouldn't aggravate her. She stepped out into the kitchen to find the door to Effie's room ajar and an abandoned mug of half-drunk tea on the table. She peered into her sister's room, frowning as she scanned the empty chamber, bedspread turned down and curtains drawn across the window. If not for the abandoned mug, she would have assumed her sister had been out all night. In the lead-up to the ceremony, the evenings grew thick with the sounds of revelry emanating from the islanders' camps. Vanna might have ventured out herself to sample the festivities if not for the injury hobbling her.

Vanna had hoped she and Effie would have the long march to the Moonflow Lagoon to catch up and spend some quality time together. No matter what newfound purpose had bolstered her sister's spirits over the last week, Vanna knew this day would still be hard for her. She'd planned to stand by in stoic support—to be whatever Effie needed her to be—but that was going to be difficult if her sister was nowhere to be found.

Vanna packed a satchel with the day's supplies and forged out on foot to join the caravan already forming at the village's edge. The wagons carrying the Ascendants and their chaperones from Sire Ansel's household staff were already trundling down the northward path, and the rest of the caravan bled into their wake, stirring into an ordered line from the busy conglomeration outside the village gates.

Vanna slipped past a small band of Nimbions in their traditional straw hats and joined an eager gaggle of Volturnians helping to load an yakcart with unopened casks of wine. She scanned for Effie as she continued to work her way through the crowd, until Raji and two of his fellow flight-suited dragoons dropped from the sky to land in her path.

"How you feeling, Lieutenant?" Raji asked.

"Like I got kicked by a horse," Vanna said.

Raji's lips turned down. He reached out and awkwardly patted her arm. She stared at his hand until he withdrew. "Suppose you won't be winging ahead with the rest of us?"

"Not this time," Vanna confirmed. The pitying look on her flier made her bristle. *This must be how Effie feels all the time.* "It's all right," Vanna said, affecting an easy grin. "The walk will do me good."

Raji opened his mouth to say something, hesitating before finally asking, "Where's your sister?"

Vanna shook her head. "She beat me out of the house this morning. Once the caravan gets underway, would you mind scanning the line for me and seeing if you can't pick her out?"

Raji nodded. "Aye-aye, Lieutenant."

Vanna sighed as she watched their images recede overhead. Without Effie or her fellow dragoons, it was going to be a long, lonely walk.

It took the better part of an hour for the rest of the gathered Zephyri to join the caravan. Vanna lingered at the back of the pack, hoping to catch a glimpse of her sister that never came. She finally fell in line behind a small group of women from the Spurs who chatted incessantly, hardly pausing to breathe.

In previous years, the caravan stretched so long that it nearly connected the village to the jungle in one unbroken chain. This year, the crowd felt thinner. The Ascension list from Volturnus had included fewer names than ever before, and Vanna supposed that might be the same throughout the archipelago, but it shouldn't have had such a profound impact on attendance. The delegations from Nimbion and Avernus arrived with the same number of kite-ships as they had in years past. Even the Spurrians presented in their typical strength.

As she worried over the vexing discrepancy, a flier glided back over the caravan to drop down at her side. Kendy fell silently into stride beside her, an unusually tight set to his jaw—especially considering the occasion.

Vanna prodded him with an elbow. "Does the caravan seem kinda *slight* to you?"

He nodded gravely. "The zeppelin from Aeolus never arrived."

Aeolus. How could she have been so daft? Vanna hadn't seen a single Aeolian all week. The windward island typically sent the second largest delegation after Volturnus.

"I just spoke to the Wing Commander of Avernus," Kendy said. "The Aeolians were two days behind his delegation. They were supposed to make landfall days ago."

"Maybe they hit rough air? Had to wait it out."

Kendy shook his head. "Bolo doesn't think so." He checked the

Spurrian group a few paces ahead to make sure no one was listening in and lowered his voice. "I don't like it, Vanna. Hal and Prestor were supposed to return on that blimp."

With that reminder, Vanna suddenly shared her commander's apprehension. "What are we going to do about it?" she whispered.

"Nothing right now," Kendy said. "We'll be too easily missed at the Ascension. But after the ceremony, I want to take a wing out west to investigate. If we don't find anything, we'll finish the crossing to Aeolus and see what we can learn."

Vanna began to nod her agreement then paused, remembering her injury. "The menders say I'm not ready to fly…"

"Then *get* ready," Kendy said, sharper than she'd heard him before. "I'll need you, Lieutenant."

Vanna bit down on her lip, nodding again. Kendy took it for confirmation and sailed off along the caravan's dusty line.

Fell tidings. Vanna knew a bit about the situation on Aeolus. Hal and Prestor sent back regular reports from the ground. Halle had been true to her word. She banished Bael and Sparrowhawk from the island, and the two pirates reportedly left without a fuss. Maybe they came back to take their revenge. Pirates weren't exactly known for their grace in defeat. Kelestina had yet to appoint a new Patrician governor, so the island's elders set up an interim council to restore some semblance of order to the disrupted shipyards and the embargoed port. Aeolus would be easy pickings for piracy without a Celestial magistrate standing guard.

All the dire possibilities cycled through Vanna's mind as the caravan crossed through the small strip of jungle and deposited the Zephyri on the cliffs overlooking the Moonflow Lagoon. With no immediate recourse, Vanna set the issue of the missing Aeolians aside and returned to the task of locating Effie.

Supply carts lined up at the jungle's edge, unloading passengers and wares. The rest of the orderly caravan spilled into a disaggregated crowd, the most eager Zephyri among them already jockeying for the best views at the cliff's edge. Vanna's bruises complained as she pressed her way through the thickening mob of onlookers, eyes searching for a tell-tale flash of purple hair. She worked her way across the gathering—from the sprawling mass of Volturnians to the straw-hatted Nimbions keeping their own company at the far end of the cliff. Eventually, the crowd grew so dense that

Vanna could no longer force her way any further without enduring substantial pain. She gave up the search with a groan of frustration.

Was it possible Effie hadn't come at all? That suddenly seemed the most likely outcome to Vanna. Perhaps her sister got up early to avoid the caravan's assembly and dodge any awkward questions. It wasn't like Effie to hide, but for all her stoic performance, standing here among the Giftless—a spectator in her year of Ascension... It might have been too much to bear.

Vanna smiled sadly to herself, content with the hope that her sister had found a place of safety on this day. It wasn't fair, but fairness so rarely factored in the Jokai's capricious design. If her sister chose to sit this one out, Vanna didn't begrudge her that peace. Effie's spirit had taken so many undeserved wounds in the last year. She seemed like she was healing but asking her to watch the Ascension she'd been summarily denied would only open them anew.

Vanna felt the pressure of the crowd building behind her, heard excited murmurings as Kelestina's procession appeared in the northern sky. Their host's gilded carriage pulled into view, drawn by her majestic hippocampi—each one piloted by a uniformed Patrician lord. Vanna strained on her toes to peer down into the lagoon. The pod of dauphine gloried in their leisure, pink and purple flippers knifing through the moonflow as they cackled at each other in good humor. Sleek cetacean bodies darted between the landing and the open air beyond, plunging beneath the ether only to emerge blasting fountains from their blowholes. The alpha floated confidently on its back, white belly glistening with moonflow. The lagoon rocked with its weight as it rolled upright, sending its subordinates to scatter.

She counted ten Ascendants bunched between the cliffside cave and the lagoon. *So few*—and five of them Volturnian. Two from Nimbion, two from Avernus, and one from Lonely Spur. When she clocked Kai's sandy head bobbing overtop his cohort, the fist of anxiety inside her chest loosened its grip. He stood motionless, eyes fixed on the Leviathan and the near-impossible task that lay before him. Kendy's niece, Min, lingered at his shoulder, while Seulin, Jaffe, and Lya helped each other stretch off to the side.

The relief proved short-lived. Kelestina's procession landed on the opposite side of the cliff, and the fist in Vanna's chest tightened once again as her eyes found one of her host's attendants.

Sire Muldoon.

The dispossessed Governor of Aeolus sat atop his hippocampi looking in much better condition than when she'd left him. He'd shaved his scruff down to a pointy goatee and he wore a fresh suit of uniform livery. His lank brown hair was now washed and conditioned to a bouncy sheen. So manicured and coiffed, he seemed even more youthful than he had on Aeolus—decades younger than his nearest Patrician peer. She watched him dismount behind Sire Ansel and take his place in the line beside their host as the Governor of Volturnus cried the ceremony to order.

Still watching Muldoon, Vanna went down to one knee with the rest of the spectators.

"Her Lightness the Celestial Kelestina," Ansel announced. "Host of the Zephyr Isles and Lady Paramount of Aquilon Palace."

Kelestina stepped forward in all her porcelain grace and raised her hands. White sun flared on the crown of her quartzite head. She fanned her fingers, and the teardrop points of her nails caught the same light, razor tips gleaming. When she spoke, her voice was like the ringing of a crystal bell. "Rise, my honored guests. We gather on the occasion of the dauphine's sojourn to bear witness to the Fourteenth Ascension of the Zephyr Isles."

Vanna watched Muldoon with such intensity that she hardly noticed a cloaked body shoving its way through the crowd to stand at her shoulder.

"Since my court arrived on Aquilon to deliver these islands from perdition, we have used this ceremony not only as a means to identify the rare Gift required to pilot Leviathan, but to mark the maturation of your sons and daughters—to induct them into their majority as accounted members of the Celestial plebiscite..."

As Kelestina's familiar speech wore on, Vanna felt the cloaked figure pressing up against her, uncomfortably close. She spared an irritated glance over her shoulder. A dark green hood concealed the top half of the man's face, but beneath the sharp lines of an aquiline nose, the ends of a blue mustache quirked to match her scowl. The fist in Vanna's chest clenched so tightly then that her heart nearly froze.

"*You!*"

A hand shot out from the cloak to squeeze her arm. "*Shh-shh-shhhh,*" Bael cautioned. "We wouldn't want to interrupt our host."

Vanna saw a few of the nearest spectators eyeing her outburst with reproach, so she turned her head back to Kelestina. "What the hell do you think you're doing here?" she whispered through gritted teeth. "I thought Halle had you banished."

"Aye," he whispered back, accent apparent even in these hushed tones. "Banished from *Aeolus*. The Wing Commander didn't say anything about the rest of the archipelago."

Kelestina finished acknowledging the Giftless sixteen-year-olds as they received their plaudits and congratulations.

"Don't draw attention," Bael said, softly applauding with four fingers against the palm of one hand. "Play along."

Vanna's jaw clenched even tighter as she clapped politely with the rest of the spectators. "Give me one reason why I shouldn't scream," she said as the applause died down.

"I wouldn't do that." She felt the point of something press against her back.

"Are you mad?" Vanna hissed. "Half the dragoons in the archipelago are here, and I've seen what Kelestina does with pirates. You'll never make it out alive."

"Maybe so." Bael pressed closer. She could feel his hot breath on her ear. "But then again, neither will you." He pushed the blade harder against her lower back then suddenly withdrew. "Relax, Lieutenant. I'm not here to make trouble. I only came to watch."

Vanna thought that unlikely, but Kelestina's presentation had already reached its conclusion. The Celestial filed back inside her carriage as her Patrician retinue mounted their hippocampi. Ansel cracked his reins, and his mount trumpeted a piscine whinny as the cavalcade descended the cliff to greet the Ascendants.

Vanna felt Bael's hand lingering at her elbow. Panic surged through her, but what could she do? The ceremony was under way.

29

EFFIE

Cramps shot through Effie's legs. They hurt so badly she had to bite her lip to keep from screaming.

She'd been crouching in a small alcove inside the moonflow cliffs for half the day, hidden behind a curtain of vines. She'd already finished the meager ration of jerky she brought along, and her canteen was nearly empty. Her stomach complained about the oversight, but the only sustenance left to her was the small vial of Nectar she'd stolen from Ava's pit, and she wouldn't be consuming that until the moment was ripe.

Between the vines, she had a decent view of the Ascendants and the pod of dauphine at their leisure in the lagoon. She assumed Kelestina's arrival when the muffled sounds of the crowd above her quieted.

Get on with it! The anticipation was agony, and not just because of the cramps.

She had an excellent view of the Ascendant cohort, smaller this year than ever before. A pair of Nimbions in dragoon flight suits lurked at the back of the pack—close enough to Effie's hiding place that she caught bits and pieces of their private conversation. Another two dragoons from Avernus traded nervous pleasantries with a plump black-haired girl from Lonely Spur. Strangely, she didn't see a single flier representing Aeolus. That alone nearly accounted for the smaller cohort.

Effie watched Kai watching the Leviathan, his gaze unbroken, sandy hair dancing to the rhythm of the winds. Min Baris lingered anxiously at his shoulder, but she seemed to know better than to break his concentration. Seulin, Lya and Jaffe looked more relaxed. They paced the edge of the lagoon's steep approach, trading jibes and helping each other stretch.

At last, Kelestina's carriage plunged into view, and the Ascendants all broke from their respective activities to attend her. Effie crept cautiously forward on her perch, cupping one ear to listen to their host's instructions.

"...You will approach one at a time in an order of your choosing. A word of caution: do not attempt to master the Leviathan by force. You come here as *petitioners*—do not forget that. As you attempt to prove your worth, you may draw upon your Gifts but remember *humility*. Leviathan choose their Pilots and not the other way around. If a dauphine finds you fit to pilot, it will offer an exchange of bows. Return the gesture as you would in my presence, but do not break eye contact as you approach. The dauphine will hold its bow and permit you to mount. If any of you successfully mount, you will still need to demonstrate *control*. Attempt to execute a piloting command, and if the dauphine complies, your Ascension will be complete. Instruct the dauphine to deliver you back to the lagoon and my retainers will receive you." The Celestial then indicated the six Patrician lords standing by in silent vigil. "Know that you have my blessing and my support as you make your approach. The Crystal Throne is depending on you—all of you—to *succeed*. Now, step forward to receive my mark."

Effie nearly tumbled from her perch as she strained to watch each Ascendant kneel before Kelestina. Their host *lowered* herself to each of them, pressing her crystalline head against their brow and whispering short sentiments for their ears alone. The contact invigorated each Ascendant as, one-by-one, Kelestina cast them off to fall in line at the lagoon's approach.

Once the last Ascendant had received their blessing, the Patricians mounted their hippocampi, and Kelestina returned to her carriage to watch the ceremony with the rest of her guests from atop the cliffs.

Silence descended on the lagoon once Kelestina's carriage vanished. Effie adjusted herself to take some of the pressure off her screaming thighs and dared to part the curtain of vines for a better view.

She assumed Kai would claim the first position, but he circled away from the approach, placing himself at the back of the queue. That left one of the Nimbion dragoons to break the ice.

The girl discarded her straw hat revealing a head of pink braids lined up in tight little rows. She gusted up the landing and began to pace the shore of the lagoon, sizing up three of the smaller dauphine floating lazily across the moonflow. One of the dauphine sighted the petitioner and drifted over, curious. It probed the Nimbion with one black cetacean eye as she drew upon her Gift to hover several feet above the ground. The display further piqued the creature's curiosity, and it drifted closer to shore, flippers lying flat across the moonflow's surface as its propeller flukes churned. The Nimbion drifted out over the moonflow, cautiously approaching her quarry. She reached out to touch the dauphine's bottlenose, and the creature spat a fountain of opalescent ether from its blowhole. The sudden blast startled the flier off course. As she lost control of her Gift, the dauphine rolled to one side and swatted her out of the air with its flipper. The Nimbion tumbled from the sky, rolling halfway down the approach before skidding to stop.

Effie exhaled her tension along with the Ascendants. Another failure. Only nine more to go.

As expected, the other Ascendants met with the same bad luck. Seulin became the first Volturnian to make her approach. She sailed out beyond the edge of the island and attempted to lure a handsome blue specimen showering in the moonflow falls. The dauphine shot forth like a lance, nearly spearing her with its bottlenose.

Lya caught a flipper to the gut that knocked the wind out of her, and Min nearly drowned herself in ether attempting to tame one of the swimmers.

Jaffe at least had a novel approach. She skated across the surface of the lagoon, propelling herself with her Gift and dragging one toe to cut balletic patterns in the moonflow. Three curious dauphine swam over and began to circle the performance, but their curiosity quickly turned violent. They circled in tighter and tighter formation, churning up a whirlpool that nearly dragged Jaffe under. The crowd gasped as the flier disappeared in a mass of pink cetacean bodies and gasped again with relief when she shot out from the center, catching a fluke to the head as her body arched back to shore.

Another year of failure seemed imminent. The rejected Spurrian girl stalked back to the cliffside dripping with moonflow, and Kai finally stepped into the first position—the archipelago's final offering for the year —or so everyone assumed.

Kai bounced on his heels, the moment's pressure building until the anticipation finally boiled over. He shot up the landing on a gust of wind and launched himself into the center of the lagoon. He landed with a splash, and the dauphine scattered, cackling wildly, hacking flippers churning the moonflow to foam. The lurking alpha took notice and sailed over from the falls, descending into the lagoon and sending up a great wave of ether. With its subordinates still stirred to frenzy, the alpha approached Kai's point of entry, prodding the surface with its bottlenose. With another great splash, Kai shot out of the lagoon on his Gift, dripping moonflow and drawing air currents against his back to buffet his climb. His body froze in mid-air, hovering eye-to-eye with the alpha.

The two stared at each other for what seemed like an eternity. Effie kept waiting for the Leviathan to reject him, but the alpha only held Kai's gaze, meeting the challenge. Its bottlenose parted, revealing a long arch of needle teeth. Careful to maintain eye contact, Kai slowly lowered his head.

All the air seemed to drain from the lagoon. Effie realized she hadn't taken a breath since Kai plunged beneath the moonflow. Still holding, she watched the alpha, motionless as it appraised Kai's bow. The alpha's line of teeth suddenly parted. The dauphine shelled Kai with a stream of clicks as it extended its flippers and began to claim altitude. Kai held his bow and his eye contact, but the alpha only continued its ascent. Flukes spinning in a blur, the dauphine climbed until its position blocked the afternoon sun.

A long shadow crept over Kai—to the shoreline and beyond. Kai broke his bow to lift his head, but too late. He sputtered out of position, attempting to brace. The alpha plummeted back to the surface, battering Kai with its bottlenose before landing in the moonflow with a terrific splash.

Kai emerged from the lagoon moments later, gasping for air as he fought the alpha's wake to paddle painfully back to shore. Once he pulled himself to dry land, he rolled onto his back, cradling his stomach and writhing in pain. Seulin and Jaffe gusted over to help him back to his feet.

Effie heard the groans of disappointment from the crowd above her.

They all thought it was over. Another year without a Pilot among them.

As Seulin and Jaffe helped Kai hobble back to safety, Effie produced the vial of Nectar she'd secreted in her cloak and pulled out the stopper with her teeth. The mixture smelled bitter like its moonberry precursor, but with an earthy, animal musk lacing its bouquet. These sweeter notes reached out from the glowing vial to prickle Effie's nostrils. A remnant recollection of her exchange with the Jokai surfaced in her mind. She saw an image of a twisted creature crouched over Ava's pit—heard the obscene trickle of its urination. Effie shook her head to banish the memories. With one last glance into the vial, she pinched her nose and swallowed its contents in one gulp.

The effect was instantaneous. The cramping claws tearing at her thighs relinquished their hold, and the hollow grumbling of her stomach stilled. The Nectar worked its arcane changes to satisfy her every bodily need. With a bitter aftertaste haunting her palate, her other senses began to sharpen. The swelling sounds of the waning ceremony blended with the rich scents of the humid lagoon. All the fresh input overwhelmed her—threatened to topple her from her perch. As she steadied herself, the colors of the day became saturated, and Effie spared a brief moment to gape at the setting's majesty with dilated eyes.

Flexing her hands, she slipped out from her covered alcove and began descending the sheer side of the cliff. She found each hand- and foothold blindly, scrambling with alacrity until her toes scraped solid ground. So exposed, she felt her time to interject herself into the ceremony running short. The failed Ascendants were already packing up, drifting toward the cave that would deliver them back to their waiting family and friends atop the cliffs. Not one of them had noticed her creeping, but that wouldn't last for long.

Effie turned her head, scanning along the lagoon's approach—fixed her gaze on the dauphine pleasantly returning to graze, expecting no further interruption. She walked toward them, picking up speed as she climbed the approach.

From their elevated vantage, the spectators noticed the intrusion before the other Ascendants. Effie heard voices heckling from the cliffs.

"Look!"

"There's someone down there!"

"...who is that?"

"Another Ascendant..."

"...not on the list."

"That's Effie Strait!"

Commotion built, voices blurring as she entered a torrid sprint.

Humped backs of every pink and purple hue rolled on the horizon like floating hilltops—drifting, growing. Wind whipped Effie's hair as she continued to accelerate. She reached the edge of the lagoon and launched herself from the shore without breaking stride.

For the first time in her Giftless life, she knew what it felt like to fly.

Body bent in a perfect dive, Effie soared, and the Moonflow Lagoon rose up to meet her. Pressure swelled inside her ears. The muffled sounds of baffled onlookers vanished as Effie plunged through the ether.

Warmth from the moonflow prickled through her skin. She opened her eyes to motes of light churning around her. Resistance slowed her descent until she finally leveled off, suspended in liquid light. The ether felt more buoyant than water and more threatening. Its currents possessed their own mercurial will. She sensed the dauphine's disturbed motion above her.

Cetacean bodies swept across the surface of the lagoon, stirring the moonflow and her floating body with it. The first adventurous dauphine dipped its head beneath the ether to investigate, and its siblings soon followed. Effie felt herself juggled between their currents as pink and purple bodies swam down to greet her.

New sensations exploded to life, each one a little earthquake inside her mind. She *felt* the dauphine's naive curiosity. A dozen dauphine circled her in nose-to-tail formation. The moonflow's density translated their cackling into song.

"*What is it?*"

Effie heard the question in her mind as clearly as if it had been whispered in her ear.

"*Another one—kin to all the rest.*"

"*Kin, perhaps, but different.*"

"*Yes.*"

Effie's lungs began to plead for air, but a vortex shaped by her encirclement dragged her down toward the bottom of the lagoon. She swam desperately against the dauphine's current, but even bolstered by the Nectar, her arms weren't strong enough to overcome the tug.

"*It struggles.*"

"*Will it die?*"

"*I don't know.*"

Help me! Effie screamed inside her mind.

Her vision began to darken around the edges as she sunk deeper. She saw two of the dauphine break formation, felt a smooth head applying pressure beneath her, nudging her against the vortex's draft. She choked through her first gasp of air as the dauphine helped her breach the surface.

Still coughing, Effie flailed, splashing wildly, Leviathan thoughts still glancing through her mind. Her head bobbed beneath the surface only to burst free with another desperate gasp. She caught a glimpse of a line of bodies along the shore watching her struggle, Kai's tall silhouette among them. If they called to her, she couldn't hear them. She paddled herself around, searching for the dauphine that saved her, but the pod had withdrawn. The lagoon's surface went suddenly still but for the weak currents of her own thrashing.

Effie settled herself enough to look up at the open sky beyond the island's edge. Her eyes tracked an impossible sight: the entire pod of dauphine had withdrawn from the lagoon. They hovered now—just beyond the island's edge—arranged in perfect risers of overlapping cetacean bodies that seemed to stretch to the horizon. Ignoring the commotion behind her, Effie caught her breath and began to paddle for the opposite shore. The dauphine bobbed in formation, watching as one.

Effie swam across the lagoon and hoisted herself back to dry land. Trailing droplets of glittering ether, she followed the path of the moonflow's spill to the point where it fed the eternal falls. She only stopped once she teetered at the island's edge—points of her toes extending out over bare sky.

A hundred Leviathan eyes stared down at her from a wall of floating bodies.

"Effie!" Kai's voice—so distant. "Come back! *Please!*"

Effie ignored him. She tried to find the dauphine voices in her mind, but the pod had gone silent in their formation.

A blast of warm wind rose up from the open sky, pressing against Effie's feet and scattering her hair in a violet cloud around her head. Cetacean bodies rippled and rolled, opening a seam at the center of their formation. The broad face of the alpha appeared through the gap, drifting through the throng of subordinates on spinning flukes. Effie felt the creature's massive weight bearing down on her. She lifted her eyes to meet its gaze, but she did not bow.

If the dauphine voices had prickled her mindscape with points of light, then the alpha's was a burning star.

"*Child of Zephyr,*" it droned.

Effie reeled. The heat of its voice made her head throb and her eyes water.

"*Unnatural,*" it burned. "*Swollen with power like a windblain sore. I could lance it... make you burst.*"

You won't. Effie's thoughts issued forth with the cadence of a command.

The alpha tipped its bottlenose, withdrawing several feet from the shoreline. "*How...*" Its body bent with a sudden spasm. Effie felt a surge of dismay from the creature—its resistance flaring and yielding, voice droning in the back of her mind. "*What is this? What do you require of us?*"

Rushing winds continued to whip Effie's hair in a long tail behind her. She pushed aside a single strand that covered her face and stared into the alpha's toothy snout.

Bow to me, she sent. *I require that you bow.*

The alpha thrashed, erupting with a stream of agitated clicks, but Effie held her ground. She felt every weakening pang of the dauphine's resistance as she drew it, thrashing, back toward the shore.

Bow to me.

Tugging like a fish on an angler's line, the alpha drifted within arm's reach.

You will bow, Effie sent.

With one jerking convulsion, the dauphine's body stilled. For a dangerous moment, she thought the Leviathan might break through her commandment in one final act of defiant will, but the alpha only clacked its bottlenose, mind quivering with resignation as it finally bent its head.

Effie reached out her hand and, sensing no further resistance, lay her fingers across its pink snout. She stroked its skin—smooth in one direction and rough in the other. The tension in this great beast bled away through her fingertips. It cooed pleasantly in response to her gentle touch. Effie yielded her ground as the alpha drifted over the island and came to rest on the shore, head bent—inviting her to mount.

"*Do not press so ardently, Child of Zephyr,*" the dauphine sent. "*I am old and you are young. It would not do for us to share a bond.*"

Effie cast her gaze out to the pod still floating overhead. *Perhaps one of your children would suit?*

"*Perhaps...*" She felt the strain of the Leviathan's consideration through their linked minds. "*But we are not the ones for you, I do not think.*"

No, Effie agreed. Her deepest instincts confirmed that the Leviathan spoke true. *But I will require your services for a demonstration.*

The alpha nodded its wide head. *"As you wish."*

In that moment, Effie felt the consciousness of each dauphine in the pod reach out to touch her mind. No words formed at their points of impact. It was rather like an internal joining of hands as the dauphine formation blasted apart into a swarming murmuration. At Effie's urging, the alpha broke from her side and plunged below the island's surface and out of sight.

Effie turned back to the lagoon. She saw the awe-struck faces of the ten failed Ascendants all watching from the opposite shore. Kai stood at their center, taller than the rest, a look of shock and adulation on his face like she hadn't seen in years.

Effie smiled for all of them, then winked just for him. She counted out seven steps back toward the lagoon then turned, sprinted for the shoreline, and dove off the edge of the world.

30

VANNA

Vanna shared in the spectators' silence, but hers was not an equal portion. Her silence had to overpower all the thoughts screaming through her head, banging on the walls of her skull with sharp-knuckled fists. They pushed her to cry out, to run—to draw upon her Gift and gust down to Effie's side. She could save her sister—from the Leviathan and herself and whatever terrible consequence awaited this profane, impulsive act. Vanna knew her sister had been plotting something, but never in her wildest imaginings could she have predicted *this*.

Effie stood at the edge of Volturnus with a wall of Leviathan lined up before her like a Celestial legion attending their officer's address. Gasps swelled within the crowd as the dauphine stirred to frenzy, and the alpha took off from the shoreline to vanish below the island's crust. She watched Effie turn to the Ascendants across the lagoon—her sister's expression occluded by distance—and Vanna kept silent still. She felt herself reaching for her sister as Effie turned on her heels and darted for the island's edge. At last, she did cry out as Effie dove beyond the island's shoreline to drop through open sky.

Vanna's knees buckled as she watched her sister plummet. Her wheezing agony became lost in blasts of shock and elation from the crowd. Panting, with her face turned down, she punched the ground until her knuckles cracked and bled. To fall over bare sky—it was the worst fate imaginable—the greatest torture on the face of Ciel.

The crowd erupted again as Vanna blinked back tears. *Don't vomit!* She swore at herself, choking down her gorge. She felt Bael's hand catch beneath her armpit. He hauled her back to her feet, and Vanna had no strength to resist. Vision blurring, she swept her head from side to side.

"Get a hold of yourself!" Bael grabbed her by the arms and shook. "Look!"

He turned her limp body to face the lagoon and pointed her teary eyes beyond the edge of the cliff. Backlit by the afternoon sun, the lagoon's image resolved slowly, and as it did, all remnant sanity vanished from the day.

It wasn't possible—a trick of the glare—or else her sister's plummet had cracked her fragile mind. But if the vision before her was a hallucination in truth, then it was a hallucination shared by all. Across the clifftop, spectators stared into the cup of the lagoon with the same open-mouthed expressions of disbelief and abject awe.

Vanna edged forward, shaking her head. *It can't be...*

Beyond the island's edge, the alpha dauphine reappeared, rising above the surface with its frenzied pod overhead. Propeller flukes spun. Flippers battered the air like oars. On its back, rode Effie.

Vanna jerked away from Bael's grasp and rubbed her eyes with the heels of her hands. Her sister stood atop the Leviathan's back, her long hair whipping behind her. The dauphine continued to climb, and Effie extended her arms in cruciform. At some unspoken command, the swarming pod moved swiftly back into formation—flying in a ring overhead, circling the alpha, adorning Effie's flight like an unbroken crown.

The wash of relief pushed Vanna to laugh through her lingering tears.

"Now, that's something you don't see every day..." Bael's voice reached her ears. "Friend of yours?"

Vanna sniffed. "She's my *sister.*"

Bael responded with a thoughtful grunt.

She'd done it.

Diminished by circumstance—denied at every turn—Effie had taken matters into her own two hands. Her own two *Gifted* hands.

Kelestina's carriage sailed back down into the ravine. Still standing, Effie piloted the dauphine to receive her. The alpha landed on the lagoon's opposite shore and bent its head to facilitate her dismount. It waited patiently like a broken mare, massive body heaving at rest with steady breaths. With the Ascendants looking on from a cautious distance, Effie met their host along the shore of the lagoon and bent her head in a respectful bow—the same bow she had denied the Leviathan.

Vanna couldn't hear the words that passed between them, but when they concluded, Kelestina welcomed her sister into a crystal embrace.

The crowd had grown quiet again—quiet enough that she heard Bael clicking his tongue.

"That's not going to be good for her," he mused.

The warning didn't land until Vanna finished watching Effie disappear into their host's gilded carriage. She turned to him, then. "What do you mean?"

His hood shifted as he shook his head. "Your sister's property of the Crystal Throne now. I think she'll find the status more stifling than her life as a mere *guest*."

Vanna turned to watch Kelestina's carriage sail off—pulled by six hippocampi—down the northway to Aquilon Landing and the palace beyond. No concluding sentiments. No further fanfare or ceremony. No acknowledgment that a Giftless plebeian had—*at last*—completed her Ascent. Vanna tried to remember what had happened the last time a Zephyri Ascended, but it was so long ago, and she had been so young...

The only thing she did remember: no one in the archipelago had seen the Pilot since.

EPILOGUE: KLAEDA

The Crimson Barnacle crackled with the noise of too many outlaw patrons with too much coin in their pockets and idle hands eager to spend it.

The pirate landing stretched the entire flat expanse of a solitary island that surfaced at unusual height in the Doric Sky. The lowest landing sat 10,000 feet above the meridian—an altitude only Leviathan could reach. That meant the Barnacle catered to an exclusive clientele. The elevation had the added benefit of keeping the bar's opaque proprietors in business. It was getting harder every year to avoid the many uniformed interests playing at authority over the open skies, and the Barnacle felt that squeeze as keenly as its outlaw patrons.

Klaeda cringed as one of Fulmina's belches reached her ears from across the bar. The swashbuckler busied herself attempting to outdrink an Avian from the Red-Tail Clan likely three times her weight. Jaim's fleshy rump overflowed from an adjacent barstool, while his balding head bobbed along to petty conversation with a sailor Klaeda recognized from Whitefang's crew. Even Cak had found kinship among a small murder of crows. They huddled together over a bucket of seed, trading squawks and flapping ruffled wings in agitated chatter. The twins were nowhere to be found. They'd vanished as soon as Tortuga made port. Klaeda could only assume they'd resurface once they finished emptying their purses at dice. Dindo hustled arm-wrestling over a barrel converted to a pitch, and Stellan courted a well-dressed Brundisian blonde who was either selling herself or fixing to rob him.

Everyone seemed to be having a grand old time. Everyone except for Klaeda, of course. A captain's work was never done.

She nursed a mug of dishwater ale, chewing her tongue impatiently as she listened to the fresh-faced whelp across the table make his case. The kid had a gloomy look about him. He hunched beneath a knit poncho, black hair roosting like a flock of skygulls, covering half his face and one of his eyes. He didn't look like much of a sailor, but he'd found his way to the Barnacle, and that was something.

"I'm not looking to buy *passage*," he said for the second time. "I want to join your crew."

"I already told you—I don't take charity cases." Klaeda reached under her hat to scratch her head. Was that a louse? Frowning, she plucked the mote from her scalp, inspected it, and flicked it away. "Every man, woman, and *child* on Tortuga is expected to earn their keep."

The boy's expression grew even more morose as he grumbled, "I can take care of myself."

"Well, whoop-dee-doo!" Klaeda slammed her hands against the table, jarring him from self-pity to open scorn. "Don't care a speck of milk from a new mom's tit what you can do for yourself, kid. The question is: what're you gonna do for *me*?"

The kid sighed, then straightened on his seat. He leaned over the table conspiratorially, expecting Klaeda to meet him halfway. She didn't oblige. "I'm Gifted," he whispered.

Klaeda blinked. "How fun for you."

"I can be useful to you," he insisted. "My Gift got me all the way here. If you just gave me a chance—to prove myself..."

Blah-buh-dee blah blah blah. Klaeda took a long sip from her mug as he prattled on. The Barnacle's ale tasted like sweat from a hostler's ass, but it was better than the rum. Fast approaching boredom, she cut him off. "Enough of that. In my experience, Gifted sailors don't usually work out. There are exceptions, of course, but you're flying against a strong current."

"What do you mean by that?" The kid sounded almost offended.

Klaeda reached under her hat to scratch her head again. "It's all too easy for your kind. You never have to fight for anything—never learn to *struggle*."

"My *kind*—"

Klaeda slammed her palm down on the table. "Don't interrupt. I can already see that you're arrogant, and arrogance makes folk slow to learn. It doesn't matter if you can fart butterflies or shoot wine from the tip of your prick; your head's as empty as a Toranese larder, and I just don't have the patience to wait around for you to fill it."

The kid's face turned down as he slumped back in his seat. "You're wrong about me," he muttered. "I know what it is to struggle."

Klaeda tapped one finger on her glass as she studied him. "Fine, then. I'll take the bait. What's your calling?"

"I told you. I'm a sailor."

"That's not what I mean! Alchemist, Elementalist, Pugilist... what sort of Gift are we dealing with here?"

He shook his head. "There's no name for it. My Gift's one of a kind."

"I doubt that."

He leaned in again, cupping his hand over his mouth. "Maybe you need a demonstration?"

Klaeda shrugged. "I suppose I could use the entertainment, since you're offering."

Nodding, he glanced over at the bar. "What's your least favorite liquor on the shelf?"

Klaeda snorted. "You planning to transmute it into honey mead?"

"Nothing so tawdry. Just answer the question, please."

Klaeda leaned back in her chair, squinting as she considered her answer. Props for showmanship. The kid finally had her piqued. "I never really had the palate for Blackstrap Rum..."

The kid nodded, still eyeing the bar. "The black bottle with the red label?"

Klaeda nodded back.

Still watching the bar, the kid swept back his swoop of hair revealing his hidden eye, and what an eye it was.

Klaeda tilted her head as she stared at it—so unlike its golden pair; solid red upon darker red, shot through with veins and markings stranger still— broken circles like the etchings of a crosshair. Klaeda gawked at the strange disfigurement, but the kid was too focused on his task to take offense. She watched with newfound curiosity as he steadied his gaze on the shelves behind the bar. With one hand concealed beneath his poncho, he shaped a pistol with two fingers and an upright thumb.

Without warning, he whispered, "*Bang*," slamming his thumb down like a hammer.

The bottle of Blackstrap Rum shattered on its shelf—as cleanly as if it had been shot in truth. The nearest server shielded himself from the flying glass as the patrons all around him dropped to the moldy floor. When no subsequent shots rang out, the server popped back up, face red, and shouted to the bar, "No guns!"

A few patrons mumbled their agreement, scanning the bar for the gunshot's origin. Unsatisfied, they returned to their leisure, and the server began sweeping up scattered shards of glass, muttering all along. "No guns... Everyone knows the rules, and the rules say *no guns...*"

The kid turned to her with a self-satisfied smirk.

She had to give it to him—she never had seen a Gift quite like his. It wasn't every day she crossed paths with a true Erratic. Klaeda sat back stroking her chin and considered his petition anew. "Where you from?" she finally asked.

"You've never heard of it."

"Try me."

The kid shrugged. "Tiny island in a worthless archipelago. North-north-east of here—about 500 leagues."

Kleada checked her mental map of the Doric Sky. "The Zephyrs?"

The kid bent his head to her, one bushy eyebrow drifting upward. "You've been there?"

"Seen 'em labeled on a map a time or two."

He nodded. "We call our island Caye Vespus, but everyone else knows it as Lonely Spur."

"Sounds thrilling," Klaeda said. "You're a long way from home."

"Yes."

"What's your name?"

He hesitated before answering. "Javion. Javion Drake."

Before Klaeda could respond, she heard the door to the Barnacle swing open and slam against the wall of the bar. A new arrival strutted in dragging a long train of grizzled crew, each face more blistered and rotten than the last. The silence that followed his arrival came in waves, breaking progressively over every last patron until the bar seemed frozen, suspended in time. So complete was the silence, that Klaeda could hear every footfall of the newcomer's steel-toed boots as they clattered across the floor.

The newcomer swept the room with his blue-eyed gaze. Every patron it touched shrank away, attempting to blend in with the furniture. When that gaze settled on Klaeda, a pair of chapped lips spread into a predatory grin.

"Scram, kid," Klaeda said as the newcomer signaled his men to scatter and avail themselves of the Barnacle's sundry pleasures. She spoke to Javion, but her focus was elsewhere.

"What?" Javion sputtered. "After all that? Surely, I've proven my worth—"

"I said *scram*." Klaeda's tone brooked no argument, but Javion still didn't move. "You want to be crew? Crew follow orders. When I say *scram*, you best go up and get."

Nostrils flaring, Javion pushed back from the table with such petulant exaggeration that he nearly backed into the unwelcome guest coming for his seat. The kid scowled up at the lurker, but something in the man's bearing must have warned him off any additional insult percolating on his tongue. He slid away from the brewing confrontation and, with one last wounded glance at Klaeda, stalked off.

The man took the kid's abandoned seat, carabiners jangling on his belt, blue eyes piercing beneath a black shroud of untamed hair. His beard had grown out since the last time she'd seen him. Some of the scars she remembered had faded to white. It was him, though—sure as the sky was deep. Scruffier, perhaps—older, certainly—but undeniably *him*.

Maugrim Shacklebur.

Klaeda sat back, folding her arms across her chest as she crossed her legs. She kicked her foot idly as the two old acquaintances stared each other down. "You must have a ripe pair of fruits on you to show your ugly mug in here."

"You would know." Maug's chapped lips parted revealing the ivory line of teeth within. Not many pirates kept a full set like those pearly whites, but Maug always did make a point of personal hygiene. He extended his arms, parting the seam of his long black cloak and revealing a red suit of skyforge armor beneath. "What? No hug?"

Klaeda pursed her lips and spat on the floor. "Not for all the gelt in Rogerbarron's Horde."

Maug's beard shifted as he affected a lugubrious frown. "I thought you'd be happier to see me."

Klaeda didn't take the bait. "You're ranging pretty far afield. Mommy let you off the leash for being such a good little boy? No one here cares if you piss on the floor, but if you start humping my leg it's gonna cost you those aforementioned fruits."

Maug reared back on his chair and laughed heartily at the rafters. His laughter tumbled out of him like barrels cut from the back of a freighter, carrying equal parts threat and good humor. "There's the Hekky I remember. Tongue as sharp as her legendary saber."

Klaeda scowled as his laughter continued. "Did you want something? Or are you just here to spoil the mood?"

Finally recovered, Maug spread his gloved hands out over the table. "You should be more gracious. Especially when I come bearing gifts."

"Never knew you to be the gift-giving type—even when we were more *cordial.*"

"What can I say? Old age has taught me generosity—among other fine traits."

"Not likely."

Maug wagged one gloved finger. "Now, now—I think you'll want to hear what I have to say."

"Let me stop you there and save you the breath." Klaeda uncrossed her legs and placed her feet flat against the floorboards. "Seeing as I can't trust a Jokai-damned word from your sparkling mouth, anything you have to say to me is just fruit of the poisoned tree. It might look nice on the branches, but I ain't picking, savvy?"

"Oh, I wouldn't be so quick to pass up a meal." Maug spun one finger in a circle about his head. "A little birdie told me that some pretty-eyed pirate with a stupid hat was looking for a mapmaker."

Klaeda froze. The trap was obvious from leagues away, but hells if he didn't have it properly baited. She spoke very low. "What would you know about that?"

"The circles I run in? You hear a lot of interesting things."

"You got something to say to me then say it. Not here for your riddles."

Maug clicked his tongue, wagging that same damned finger. "You used to be more fun."

Klaeda grunted. "Old age has made me ornery, among other fine traits."

"Oh, I do miss you, Hekky!" That reckless laugh of his assaulted her anew.

"Then why don't you join me on Tortuga? I always like to give your kind a guided tour of the open sky." She flashed her own teeth, not half as white as Maug's but just as threatening.

"Tempting..." he mused. "But I'm afraid I have my own affairs to manage. This is just a courtesy call."

Klaeda pressed her lips back together and shrugged. "Offer stands if you ever change your mind. Now let's get down to the meat of this fish before your company does any more damage to my reputation. The cartographer —what do you know and what's it gonna cost me?"

"No price this time. I said it was a present, and presents are free. I have it on good authority that the man you're looking for is currently a guest of Her Lightness Kelestina of Aquilon."

"*Her Lightness*?" Klaeda cringed at the Celestial's mention. "I remember a time not so long ago when 'Her Lightness Kelestina of Aquilon' was the 'Shard-faced Slag of Solaris' or 'that porcelain bitch' when you were less inclined to wax poetic."

"But it *was* a long time ago," he countered. "A lifetime." Maug's composure showed the first signs of breach—a slight tightening in the skin around his eyes and a mild tremor in his upper lip. Easy to miss for someone who didn't know him better, but as obvious to Klaeda as a cannon enfilade. He leaned back, affecting nonchalance, and the skin around his eyes relaxed, restoring his mask of control. "Besides, I like to think I've matured beyond name-calling."

Klaeda folded her arms again as she considered taking a bite of Maug's poisoned fruit. "Aquilon, huh? That's a long haul."

"Tortuga not up to the task? She must be getting a little long in the tooth." He flashed his own set again—so damn proud, he was.

Ignoring the provocation, Klaeda took a sip from her mug. Time to settle and reach room temperature didn't do the Barnacle's ale any favors. She squinted at Maug over the foaming lip of her mug. "What's your angle here? And don't feed me any more of that dreck about generosity."

"Would 'for old time's sake' suffice?"

"Sure wouldn't."

"Oh, I don't know, Hekky. Life's a cocktail! Sometimes you have to stir things up a little to get the right blend." The mischievous glint in Maug's eye surfaced memories Klaeda would rather forget. "Maybe old age hasn't taught me anything, after all." He laughed again then slammed his hands down on the table and pushed back his chair. As he stood to take his leave, he straightened the lines of his long black coat. "What does it matter, anyway? You have the information I came here to deliver. Do with it as you please."

Their eyes lingered on each other for a pregnant moment, and Maug parted his lips like he was about to speak, but he must have thought better of it, because he slammed them shut and performed a mocking bow instead. "Be seeing you around the watering holes, Hekky."

"Hope not—for your sake." She watched his coattails swishing as he strutted away.

Klaeda waited for him to vanish around a bend in the bar. "Hey kid," she hollered. "Javion."

He'd been lurking nearby throughout the entire interaction, waiting for his chance to slip back in and continue pleading his case.

At the sound of her summons, he nearly tripped over his poncho in his haste to reach her side. "Yes?"

"Aquilon—that's an island in your archipelago, isn't it?"

He nodded enthusiastically. "It is, but there's nothing there except one of the Shards' palaces."

Klaeda stood up from her seat and clapped him on the arm. "Congratulations, kid. I've decided you might be of some use to us, after all."

His good eye lit up like an alchemical torch. "Does that mean…"

She nodded. "You're hired. Welcome to the Tortuga."

ACKNOWLEDGMENTS

Sending any novel out into the universe is an act of faith. This is especially true of First Novels. Keeping faith has never been a personal strength, but I've been fortunate to have many shining souls in my orbit who kept the hope alive when I lacked the strength to do so. To you all, my sincerest and tearful thanks:

First and foremost, to my loving and supportive partner, Liz, who has sacrificed at least as much as I have to the capricious Gods of the written word. To my children, Judd and Aliyah, forced to share their father's time with a panoply of fictitious siblings. To my first reader, story consultant, and oldest friend, Jon Koster, whose invaluable insights live on every page. To Dr. Corinna Most and Dr. Andrew Somerville, whose encouraging responses pushed me to take publication into my own clumsy hands. Every fantasy writer should have a world-class anthropologist on speed dial, and I have two. To my parents, who encouraged me through decades of rejection and failure and never once questioned my quixotic journey. To my brothers, Harry, Sam, and Jake, who inspire me to keep the pen in my hand with their own remarkable creative achievements. To my MFA committee, Dr. Jeremy Withers, K.L. Cook, and David Zimmerman, spectacular writers and generous readers, all. Lastly, to my Clarion instructors, Greg Frost, Geoff Ryman, Catherynne Valente, Ann Vandermeer, and Jeff Vandermeer, for tolerating my juvenilia and identifying the potential buried within.

I needed all of you to do this.

Much more to come.

ABOUT THE AUTHOR

Z. Bennett Lorimer is a graduate of the 2014 Clarion Science Fiction and Fantasy Writers Workshop at UC-San Diego. He holds an MFA in creative writing from Iowa State University and is the former managing editor of the international literary journal *Flyway: Journal of Writing and Environment*. A Long Island native, he currently lives in Ames, Iowa, with his partner and children.

FORTHCOMING BOOKS IN TALES OF CIEL

Book 2: Ophiuchus Flinched

(February 3, 2026)

Book 3: The Mark of Cain

(April 21, 2026)

WANT TO SEE WHAT HAPPENS NEXT?

Scan the QR code to download your free preview of Book 2: *Ophiuchus Flinched*.

And don't forget to sign up for the High Trestle Press newsletter by visiting www.hightrestlepress.com for weekly updates about upcoming books from Z. Bennett Lorimer.

www.ingramcontent.com/pod-product-compliance
Lightning Source LLC
Chambersburg PA
CBHW060451300726
48975CB00008B/2469